YOU WON.
I CAN'T
UNLOVE
YOU!

NAMAN MISHRA

DEDICATED TO

To the people who are lost in the ways of love, who dwell in the past and work for the future!

TABLE OF CONTENTS

|| राधे-राधे ||

ABOUT THE AUTHOR

The journey started when Naman Mishra, went for his graduation and there he met some really great people who inspired him to write, to focus on the orthodox issues prevailing in the society. Not only that, but there were also many things that took place in his surroundings which changed his way of thinking and made him more anxious to write as well as share his own personal stories.

Naman has completed his Master of Arts in Economics and also, he is working practically in the field of Economics and contributing to the same by carrying out various research. Naman is ambitious, while focusing on all issues, stigmas and stereotypes that others go through. Naman's journey continues as he uses his writing and research to inspire positive change in the world.

✉   mnaman225@gmail.com
◙   @naman_mishra5
in   @Naman Mishra

PROLOGUE

Love is often described as a fire—a blaze that consumes, a passion that burns brightly, leaving ashes in its wake. But there exists a kind of love that is quieter, timeless, and unshakable. It does not seek possession or demand to be spoken aloud. It lingers in silences, in fleeting glances, in words left unsaid. It is the kind of love that holds people together not by touch but by memory, not by proximity but by a shared understanding of the soul. This story is not about grand gestures or stolen kisses under moonlit skies. It is not about love that demands to be seen but rather love that insists on being felt—deeply, unshakably, and irrevocably. The kind of love that exists in the crevices of time, waiting patiently to be remembered. It is about the invisible threads that bind us to one another, pulling gently across the years, across lives, until we are ready to see them.

For Arjun and Meera, love was never bound to a fleeting moment of passion. It was etched in the spaces between their words, in the quiet admiration of one heart for another. It was a love that gave without asking, that nurtured without demanding. It was love as a lesson—teaching patience, sacrifice, and the art of letting go. It was the kind of love that builds people rather than binds them. And yet, life has a curious way of testing such love. Years become decades, faces change, and the weight of the world bears down on shoulders that were once free of burden.

Promises, both spoken and unspoken, are carried forward, tethering two souls even as they walk separate paths. This is the story of a bond that time could not weather, of two lives shaped not by the closeness of hands but by the intimacy of hearts. It is the journey of two people whose love was never defined by the conventional—never by what was, but rather by what could be. It is a story of loss and of finding; of separation and of belonging.

As you turn these pages, step into the quiet beauty of a love that defies the boundaries of the ordinary. Let yourself feel the weight of their silences, the depth of their longing, and the resilience of a connection that endured even as life moved on. Some loves are not meant to be lived in the flesh but are instead woven into the fabric of who we become. This is that love. A whisper across decades. A journey back to where it all began.

PART I

WHISPERS OF DAWN

CHAPTER I

THE SEAT BY THE WINDOW

The sun dawned in the sky and the early morning light filtered through the half-open curtains, casting short shadows and spreading a golden pastel across the room. In front of the mirror, Arjun stood with a quite smile playing across his lips, busy adjusting the lapel of his suit. He wondered that today was the day, the day that he had been waiting for since long. This day has been an unacknowledged and unknown part of him for a better part of his life, and alas it has arrived unceremoniously but inevitability. The day which deems his life to become a full circle. Arjun's fingers stumbled across the cufflinks, small, gold and slightly worm. These were a reminiscent of the past, belonging to his father and now after decades of being forgotten in a drawer, being used again. The chime of the metals clinking against each other when he fasted them brought over him a wave of nostalgia, a string of memories that were as familiar as the suit he wore. Today wasn't just another day—it was the day he would finally meet her again.

With a deep breath, Arjun stared at the reflection in the mirror. His salt and pepper hair was neatly combed, although the struggled against certain rebels which popped again and again. his face, although lined with age and harsh was softened with wisdom, holding a look of contentment, showing a man who has made peace with all he did and all he missed. His suit, navy blue and perfectly tailored, hugged his tall frame, bringing with it a sense of dignity that had only grown over the years. On the outside Arjun was calm, but in underneath this composure, there was a bubbling excitement, quite visible with his hands trembling slightly while be buttoned his jacket. His heart was humming loudly a bit faster he felt with each passing minute, every movement was leading him to the fated day and closure. Today, he wasn't just dressing for himself; he was dressing for a moment he had carried in his heart for more than three decades. The weight of the years seemed to lift off his shoulders, and for a brief moment, he felt like the young man he once was, filled with hope and a sense of possibility.

"Meera!" he called out, his voice echoing through the quiet house. The name seemed to hang in the air a bit longer, a name that held more meaning for him than anyone else. For him, she was everything his pride, his joy – the little girl he had raised with so much care and love. Her presence today was no less important than the day itself, it meant something more. Today, she would witness a chapter of her father's life, a chapter which she had only anticipated and heard fragments about. With the echoing name, came the soft sound of footsteps, accompanying the announcement that Meera appeared in the doorway. Meera had her hair pulled back in a loose braid but the sense of excitement in his father's voice made her curious. She was a woman, in her mid-twenties now, in her own right, but to her father she was still the young girl whom he had raised with so much care. The memory was the day was bleak, the golden day of the book fair, a faint fragment which always made him thank God for being kind.

"Papa, why are you so dressed up?" she asked, her voice soft but teasing, as if the seriousness of the moment hadn't quite sunk in for her.

Arjun turned to face her, his smile broadening. "Today's a special day, Meera. I have a meeting—one that I've been waiting for, for a long time."

Meera raised an eyebrow, crossing her arms. "A meeting? What kind of meeting requires cufflinks and a suit this early in the morning?"

Arjun chuckled softly, stepping toward her. He placed a hand on her shoulder, his gaze warm but unreadable. "Come with me. I cannot make this meeting without you! Though I have a special request for you, please watch from afar, just for a little while. It is important!"

Meera stared blankly at his father, she was confused and surprised with the seriousness of his tone. Meera was a bit taken back, but understanding that it was not the time to question, nodded in agreement. She knew her father well, he has always been true to her, but still there were parts of him, some untold parts which belong to a past which she wanted to but never dared to venture.

"I'll get ready," she said quietly, turning back toward

her room, leaving her father alone with his thoughts once more.

Arjun stood there, in the silence of the house feeling comfortable. He slowly walked towards the window , pulling the blinds open wider, allowing more light to flood the room. Outside, the world was coming to life. The birds sang softly, and the crisp morning air promised a new beginning. Everything felt right today, as if the universe itself had aligned for this moment. His mind was kept going back to the so many years back, the day where everything began. He ached at the thought of remembrance but the ache was familiar, it was an old wound that had long since healed but still remembered the sting of its origin. Arjun remembered his past, his actions, his bonds and how life turned carrying its own various paths. Arjun never regretted his life, never in reality, but in the depths of his heart there was always a part that kept on wondering. Wondering what could have been, still after all these years, he could not help it.

"Are you ready, Papa?" Meera's voice broke through his thoughts, and he turned to see her standing by the door, dressed simply but beautifully, her face reflecting curiosity and a touch of excitement.

"I'm ready," he said softly, his voice filled with quiet resolve.

Both the father and daughter duo got to the car and drove to the coffee shop, filled with a companionable silence. Arjun's mind was on the meeting, he anticipated on what would happen, what would be said. He feared what the past had in store? Would there be a familiar feeling? Would there be a same serene feeling in the meeting like always? He wasn't nervous, but there was a weight of expectation in his chest. They arrived at the coffee shop. It was a quaint, little place, tucked away from the hustle of the city, just as it had been all those years ago. Arjun parked the car and turned to Meera.

"Stay here for a moment. When I give you the signal, you can come inside and watch from the back. Just... trust me on this."

Meera, puzzled but trusting, nodded. Arjun stepped out of the car, taking a deep breath as he straightened his suit. The air was filled with the smell of freshly brewed coffee, and with it, the scent of memories long kept. He entered the coffee shop, his heart quietly racing, and took a seat by the window—the same seat they had shared all those years ago.

And then, he waited.

CHAPTER II

TANGLED SERENDIPITY

The book fair stretched across the park, with rows of tables laden with piles of book calling for various enthusiastic readers to dive into the immaculate pool of knowledge. The air was filled with scent of old paper and freshly printed ink, carrying the promise of stories waiting to told and experienced. It was the kind of place where time slowed, where the world stopped and none of it mattered more. Here, amidst all the hustle and bustle of pages, the quietness of the slow murmurs, everything in life felt simpler and a but more meaningful. Among the long aisles, Arjun wandered with his hands tucked casually into the pockets of his jacket, eyeing the various gems neatly arranged. In general Arjun was not looking anything in particular, but he wasn't the one to miss a chance to explore this enchanting world of stories. Even though Arjun's had a knack for architecture, characterized with its rigid lines and meticulous lines, the world of books is what offered him a different perspective. It gave him a place to escape, to dream, to be limitless without any boundaries and with endless possibilities.

Arjun has been this ambitious kind of person, one who always looked ahead to progress. At the age of twenty-two, he was on the cusp of graduating, already set on pursuing his higher studies abroad. His mind was full of blueprints and cityscapes, ideas of grand buildings that would one day define his career. But today, at this book fair, he was content to let his mind wander, to take a break from the future he was so carefully crafting. While trotting the sprawling lines of books, Arjun paused, his eyes fixated on a familiar title. *To Kill a Mockingbird.* The book drove him back to years ago, when he had read it, it was the simplicity and the power of story which he couldn't forget. For it was a book which stayed with him through the years, one that made any person think long even after turning the final page. He reached out to grab the book, his fingers brushing over the cover just as another hand reached for the same book.

Arjun was taken back by it, he looked up and found himself mesmerised by a pair of deep brown eyes, framed by loose stands of dark hair, carefully creasing around her face. She was about his age, maybe a little younger, with a soft, thoughtful expression that immediately made him curious. There was something in the way she stood, the way her fingers hovered over the book, that told him she wasn't just browsing—she was searching, much like he was.

"Sorry," he said, pulling his hand back with a small, embarrassed smile. "Didn't mean to interrupt."

The girl smiled, a shy, almost hesitant smile, as if she wasn't used to moments like this. "No, it's okay," she said softly. "It's a great book."

Arjun nodded, glancing at the cover again before meeting her eyes. "Yeah, one of my favorites, actually."

"Mine too," she replied, her voice barely above a whisper, but there was a warmth in her tone that made Arjun pause. There was something about her—something quiet, something deep.

"I'm Arjun," he said, extending his hand, his curiosity piqued.

"Meera," she replied, her handshake gentle but firm. "I guess we have good taste in books."

Arjun chuckled, releasing her hand and looking down at the book again. "Yeah, seems like it." He paused, not quite sure what to say next. He was used to talking to people, to being confident and forward, but something about Meera made him feel like he had to tread carefully, like she was someone who required a slower, more thoughtful approach.

"So, you're a fan of Harper Lee?" he asked, trying to keep the conversation going.

Meera nodded, her eyes lighting up a little at the mention of the author. "I love how she writes about morality and justice, but in such a simple, human way. There's so much depth in her words, but she doesn't overcomplicate it. It's just... real."

Arjun listened, fascinated by the way her voice softened when she spoke about the book, as if she were sharing a secret. It wasn't just a casual interest for her—she felt it, understood it on a deeper level. He could tell she was the kind of person who didn't just read books; she lived them, breathed them.

"Are you studying literature?" he asked, almost certain of the answer.

Meera nodded again, a small smile playing on her lips. "Yeah, final year. I'm hoping to go into research, maybe write one day."

Arjun raised an eyebrow, impressed. "That's... amazing. Writing your own books?"

She laughed softly, shaking her head. "Not yet. I think I'm still trying to figure out what I want to say, you know? I love stories, but I don't want to just write for the sake of it. I want it to mean something."

Arjun nodded, understanding more than he expected to. "I get that. I'm an architecture student, but I feel the same way about buildings. It's not just about making something that looks good—it has to serve a purpose, it has to mean something to the people who use it."

Meera looked at him, her gaze curious. "Architecture? That's... interesting. It never occurred to me that this could be interpreted as such!"

Arjun smiled. "I know! This is the general thought. But I feel that is why I like it, for me it is like weaving my own story into reality, making use of buildings rather than a quill."

The moment that followed was one which was filled in a comfortable silence. The noise of the fair seemed to be fading in the background. It felt that the conversation was a gradual and more natural one, one which was between friends who had known each other far longer than just a few minutes. Arjun couldn't understand it, but there was something about Meera that made him want to keep talking, to keep exploring whatever this was.

"I guess we're both trying to figure things out," he said after a while, his voice thoughtful. "But I think that's okay. Sometimes, the best things in life don't have to be planned. I always hope for life to give me adventures, to explore and to live!"

Meera glanced at him, baffled, curious and a bit impressed, her eyes were reading his face, as if to decide something. She wanted to but did not, she just smiled- a real smile this time, one that reached her eyes. "Yeah," she said softly. "Maybe you're right."

They continued to talk, their conversation drifting from books to life, to their hopes and dreams. Arjun told her about his plans to study abroad, about the buildings he wanted to design one day. Meera listened, her eyes thoughtful, but there was a quiet sadness in her expression, as if she were already beginning to understand that their paths were heading in different directions. As the sun began to dip lower in the sky, casting long shadows across the park, they both realized that their time together was coming to an end. There was no grand goodbye, no promises of staying in touch. They exchanged a simple look—one that held all the things left unsaid—and then they parted ways, each carrying with them the memory of a chance encounter that felt like it could have been something more.

Arjun walked away with a strange feeling in his chest, as if he had just lived through something important, something he wouldn't fully understand until much later. And as for Meera, she stood for a moment longer, watching him disappear into the crowd, before turning back to the book fair, her thoughts tangled with possibilities. They didn't know it yet, but this moment would stay with them, shaping their lives in ways they couldn't yet imagine.

CHAPTER III

UNWRITTEN LINES, UNSPOKEN BONDS

The sky was a soft, powdery blue that morning, the kind that stretched endlessly above the bustling city, offering a rare sense of calm. Arjun sat at a small café near the corner of an old street, sipping on his coffee. The smell of fresh pastries and brewing espresso filled the air. He glanced down at the book in his hand, *To Kill a Mockingbird*, the very same one Meera had let him take at the book fair. It had been a few weeks since that encounter, yet she lingered in his thoughts. There was something about her that stayed with him—not just her love for literature, but the quiet warmth in her presence, the way she seemed to understand the world in a way that felt familiar, even though they barely knew each other. He had returned to the book fair once or twice, hoping to see her again, but life had a way of pulling people in different directions. His final year in architecture school was consuming most of his time, and though he enjoyed the challenge, his mind often wandered back to Meera. There was something unspoken between them, something that didn't need words or labels, and yet it felt like the beginning of something important.

Just as Arjun turned a page, the soft sound of footsteps interrupted his thoughts. He looked up, and there she was—Meera. She had spotted him from across the street and was now standing in the doorway of the café, smiling softly as their eyes met.

"Arjun," she said, her voice full of surprise yet laced with the same familiarity they'd shared at the book fair.

"Meera," he replied, rising to his feet, unable to hide the smile that tugged at his lips.

Without saying much more, she crossed the room and joined him at the table. For a moment, they sat in a comfortable silence, each of them absorbing the serendipity of their second meeting. There was no need for grand explanations or gestures—just the quiet acknowledgment that their paths had crossed again, perhaps for a reason neither of them fully understood yet.

"Seems like fate has its way," Meera said with a light chuckle as she placed her small handbag on the table. "I didn't expect to see you here."

Arjun smiled and nodded. "Neither did I, but I'm

glad you did. It feels like we left something unfinished at the book fair."

Meera's eyes lit up with amusement. "You mean the book?"

"That, and maybe something else," Arjun said, his tone teasing but gentle.

As the conversation flowed, it became clear that their connection was deeper than just shared interests. They spoke about their studies—Meera about her growing love for literature, how she often lost herself in the words of writers from times past, and Arjun about his passion for designing spaces that told their own stories. Their worlds were different, yet complementary. Meera was introspective, more grounded in the emotional landscapes that books painted, while Arjun was always looking ahead, chasing big dreams, and imagining the structures he would one day create. They were two souls at different crossroads, yet their conversations felt effortless, as if their paths had been waiting to intertwine.

As the afternoon sun dipped lower in the sky, they found themselves walking through the city together. It became a habit after that day—meeting up whenever they could, usually at the same little café, sometimes exchanging handwritten notes when they couldn't meet in person. Meera had a way with words that moved Arjun in ways he didn't expect. Her letters were filled with poetic musings about life, love, and everything in between. They didn't speak of their growing bond in terms of a relationship; rather, they let it unfold, undefined and free, not caged by expectations or labels.

One evening, as they sat together, Arjun pulled out a small envelope from his pocket. It was one of the letters Meera had sent him. "This one," he said, holding it up, "this is my favorite."

Meera blushed slightly but smiled, curious. "Why?"

"Because it's not just words. It's you. Every time I read it, I feel like I'm getting to know you a little better," Arjun said, his voice low, a touch of seriousness creeping in.

Meera looked at him for a moment, her expression softening. "I guess that's why I write to you. There are things that are easier to say on paper. Things that take time to understand."

Their letters became more than just a form of communication—they became a part of their story. Whenever they couldn't meet, they'd write to each other, sometimes waiting days to receive a reply. There was something old-fashioned and beautiful about it, something that made their connection feel even more special. In a world that was speeding up with technology, they found solace in slowing down, in waiting, in savoring every word they exchanged. Occasionally, they would go to a nearby cyber café, where the clunky old computers hummed and buzzed as they sent emails to each other, laughing at the oddity of using such a modern tool when their hearts were so rooted in the past. Even though emails allowed for quicker exchanges, they still preferred the letters—the slow, deliberate act of writing by hand.

As the months passed, their bond deepened, though it remained undefined. There was no pressure to call it anything—no rush to put a label on what was blossoming between them. Their connection was their own, something they cherished in the quiet moments they shared at the café or in the brief exchanges of letters and emails. But there were moments, too, where they both felt the pull of reality. Arjun's studies were nearing completion, and he was preparing to leave for higher education abroad. Meera, on the other hand, was more rooted in her family, her responsibilities tying her to her home. They didn't talk about what would happen when Arjun left, not because they didn't care, but because their connection felt larger than the practicalities of time and distance.

One evening, as they sat in their favorite spot at the café, Arjun glanced at Meera, a question lingering in his mind. "Do you ever think about the future?"

Meera looked at him, her expression thoughtful. "Sometimes. But not in the way most people do. I don't think about it in terms of what will happen or what won't happen. I think about it in terms of the moments we have now. That's what matters."

Her words hung in the air between them, and Arjun felt the weight of them. She was right. The future was uncertain, but what they had now—this undefined love, this connection that defied labels—that was real. And for now, that was enough.

In the soft glow of the café lights, they sat together, not needing to say much. Their love wasn't rushed, nor was it something they felt the need to define. It was simply there, growing quietly between them, as natural as the changing seasons.

And so they continued, meeting at the café, exchanging letters, letting their love unfold in its own time, undefined but undeniable.

CHAPTER IV

LOVE DWELLS IN SILENCE

The days that followed felt like stolen moments from a time long past, an era untouched by the rush of modernity. Arjun and Meera spent hours together, though it was never at each other's homes or in any overly intimate setting. They met in parks, at bookshops, or at their favorite corner café, where the scent of freshly brewed coffee and the quiet hum of conversation made them feel as though they were suspended in time. Each moment they spent together felt pure, unhurried, and full of possibility. Their connection wasn't something they could define with words. It didn't fit into the neat boxes that most relationships seemed to demand. They never spoke of love in the traditional sense, nor did they make promises to each other. Yet, there was an unspoken understanding between them that surpassed what they could express. It was as if their hearts had already made a pact, one that didn't require declarations or commitments—just an unshakable trust in the way they felt when they were together.

On an afternoon when the sun was low and the air was crisp, Meera turned to Arjun after one of their conversations about literature. But as the conversation trailed off, she looked at him with a softness in her eyes.

"Arjun," she said quietly, her voice barely above a whisper, "do you ever wonder why we met?"

Arjun's gaze shifted to her, and for a moment, he didn't answer. He just let the question hang in the air between them, as though the answer was too profound for words. "I think," he finally said, after a long pause, "that some things are meant to happen without a reason. Maybe we're not supposed to understand it. Maybe that's what makes it special."

Meera smiled, her heart warming at his words. There was a truth in them that she couldn't deny. Every moment they spent together felt like it was happening for the first time, like they were discovering each other in new ways with every conversation, every glance. She had never felt this way before—this kind of quiet, steady affection that didn't demand anything in return.

It was pure.

The world around them seemed to fade when they were together. And in that fading, they found solace. They didn't need to speak of the future, didn't need to plan what was coming next. All they needed was the present moment, and in that moment, they were content.

One day, Meera received news that she would have

to visit her relatives for a few weeks. Her heart sank at the thought of being away from Arjun. Though they hadn't made any formal commitments to each other, she knew she would miss their time together—the way his eyes lit up when he talked about architecture, or the way he always carried a book in his bag, just in case they found a quiet place to sit and read.

"I'll write to you," Arjun said when she told him the news, his tone light but his eyes serious. "We'll find a way to stay connected."

And true to his word, Arjun did write. He sent his letters to a nearby friend of Meera's who lived close to her relatives, ensuring that his words would still find their way to her, even though they were miles apart. His letters were full of thoughtfulness and small details about his day, interspersed with musings about life and love. But beneath the surface of every word, there was something deeper—something that told Meera how much he missed her, how much he cherished the connection they shared.

In one letter, he wrote:

"Meera, I find myself thinking of you often these days. Not in a way that makes me sad, but in a way that makes me realize how much your presence brings light into my life. I miss our conversations, our walks through the city. But more than that, I miss the way you make me feel understood, without ever having to say a word. I hope you're well. I hope you know that you're in my thoughts, always."

Meera read those words in the quiet of her room, her heart swelling with an indescribable sense of joy and longing. There was something so profoundly beautiful in the way Arjun expressed himself—not in grand gestures or sweeping declarations, but in the simple act of sharing his thoughts, his day, his heart.

She wrote back to him, pouring her feelings onto the pages of her own letters, telling him how much she missed their time together, how much she cherished the connection they had, even when they were apart.

"Arjun," she wrote, *"I find myself thinking of the time we spent at the café, the way the light hit the table just right, and how, for a moment, I felt like we were the only two people in the world. There's a quiet comfort in knowing that we're both under the same sky, even if we're not together. I look forward to the day we can sit and talk again."*

When Meera returned from her relatives' home, she and Arjun resumed their meetings as though no time had passed. But something had shifted between them. Their connection had deepened in ways that neither of them could fully articulate. They didn't speak of love, not explicitly, but there was a new understanding between them—a sense that their hearts were bound together in a way that transcended the need for labels or promises.

One evening, as they walked through the park after another long conversation, Arjun stopped and turned to Meera. "Do you ever think about the future?" he asked, his voice soft, almost tentative.

Meera looked up at him, her eyes reflecting the fading light of the setting sun. "I do," she admitted, her voice equally soft. "But I don't think about it the way most people do. I think about it in terms of moments. The moments we have now, the moments we might have later. And I think... I think that's enough for me."

Her words were simple, but they carried a weight that Arjun felt deep in his chest. He reached out and took her hand, squeezing it gently. "I think that's enough for me, too," he said.

In that moment, they both understood what they

had—this love that didn't need to be named or defined, this connection that was strong enough to exist without expectations or demands. It was pure, it was wholehearted, and it was theirs. As they continued to walk, hand in hand, there was no need for more words. The love they shared was enough—more than enough. It was the kind of love that didn't ask for anything in return, the kind that simply existed in the spaces between them, quiet and steady, like the turning of the seasons.

And in those moments, they knew, without having to say it, that their hearts had found a home in each other. A home that didn't need walls or boundaries, but one that would always be there, waiting for them, no matter where life took them.

CHAPTER V

A FRAGILE INFINITY

The days had grown shorter, but somehow, the moments Arjun and Meera spent together felt longer, stretched by the weight of things unsaid. They still met at their favourite café, still exchanged letters when they couldn't meet, and still laughed about the books they read and the stories they dreamed of writing. But underneath all that joy, there was a quiet sadness neither of them dared to acknowledge. It started with small signs. Arjun would sometimes glance at his watch, his mind half-occupied with the letters of acceptance from universities abroad. His ambition had always been one of the things that Meera admired most about him. He had plans for his future, dreams that stretched far beyond the borders of their town, and she loved hearing him talk about the buildings he wanted to design, the cities he wanted to visit. Yet, with every mention of his studies, there was a flicker of doubt in her chest. What would become of them when he left?

Meera, on the other hand, had responsibilities that weighed heavily on her. Her family depended on her in ways that made it impossible to think about leaving. They weren't demands that anyone spoke of directly, but they were there, unspoken expectations that kept her anchored to her home, her town, her life. She wanted to be free, to follow her heart, but that freedom wasn't something she could grasp without breaking something precious—something she wasn't sure she could fix.

One evening, after a long walk through the city, they sat on a bench by the lake, the quiet sounds of the water lapping against the shore filling the spaces between them. Meera stared at the sky, the pale pinks and blues of the sunset reflecting in her eyes.

"Do you ever feel like we're chasing something we'll never reach?" she asked softly, her voice barely breaking the stillness of the evening.

Arjun looked at her, his brow furrowing slightly. "What do you mean?"

Meera sighed, her breath catching as she struggled to find the right words. "I mean... this. Us. Our lives. Sometimes I feel like everything is moving forward, and I'm just standing still. Like I'm waiting for something to happen, but I don't know what."

Arjun's heart clenched at her words, because he knew exactly what she meant. He had felt it too, in those moments when he was excitedly telling her about his plans for the future, only to remember that she wasn't part of those plans. Not because he didn't want her to be, but because life had a way of pulling them in different directions, and there didn't seem to be a way to stop it.

"I've thought about it," he admitted, his voice low. "I've thought about what happens next. About us."

The air between them grew heavier, the weight of his words sinking into the space they shared. Meera turned to him, her eyes searching his face for answers she wasn't sure she wanted to hear.

"I don't want to go," Arjun said, almost pleading. "I don't want to leave you behind, Meera. But I don't know what else to do. This is what I've been working for my whole life. It's what I've dreamed of."

Meera's heart broke a little more at his words, even though she knew they were true. She had always known that Arjun's dreams were bigger than this town, bigger than the life they had together. But hearing him say it aloud made it real, and the reality of it was more painful than she had imagined.

"I don't want you to stay for me," she whispered, though every part of her wanted to scream the opposite. "You deserve everything you've worked for, Arjun. You deserve to follow your dreams."

Her voice wavered as she spoke, but she forced herself to stay strong, to not let the tears that were gathering in her eyes spill over. Arjun reached for her hand, squeezing it gently, and she held on tightly, as though letting go would mean letting go of everything they had.

"What about your dreams?" he asked, his voice thick with emotion. "What about what you want?"

Meera closed her eyes for a moment, her thoughts swirling in a confusing mix of love and duty. What did she want? She wanted Arjun. She wanted a life with him, one filled with the kind of love that wasn't weighed down by responsibilities and expectations. But she also knew that wasn't possible—not for her. Her family needed her. Her life wasn't just hers to live.

"I want…" she began, her voice breaking. "I want to be free, but I don't think I can be. I have responsibilities, Arjun. My family… they need me. I can't just leave."

Arjun's grip on her hand tightened as he stared at her, his mind racing. He had always known that Meera's life was complicated, that her love for her family was strong, but he hadn't realized just how much it was holding her back. He wanted to tell her that they could figure it out, that they could make it work, but deep down, he knew it wasn't that simple.

"I don't know how to let go of you," Arjun confessed, his voice raw. "I don't want to let go."

Meera's heart shattered at his words, because she felt the same way. She didn't want to let go either, but she couldn't see a way forward for them—not without one of them giving up everything. And neither of them deserved that.

"Maybe we don't have to," she said quietly, though she didn't fully believe it. "Maybe we can just… be. Without expectations. Without plans."

It was a lie they both wanted to believe, but in the pit of their stomachs, they knew the truth. Their lives were pulling them apart, and there was nothing they could do to stop it. They were clinging to something that couldn't last, but neither of them had the courage to break it, not yet. So, instead of saying goodbye, they held on a little tighter. They continued to meet at the café, to write letters, to share stolen moments together, all the while knowing that the end was inevitable. They didn't speak of it, didn't let the reality of their situation cloud the happiness they still found in each other's company. But it was there, lurking in the shadows, waiting for the moment when they would finally have to face it.

One day, when Meera was away visiting family, Arjun sent her a letter that broke her heart a little more:

"Meera, I keep thinking about what we talked about, about the future. I don't know what's going to happen, but I do know one thing—I love you. And no matter where life takes us, that will never change. I hope you know that."

Meera read those words in the quiet of her room, tears streaming down her face. She loved him too, more than she could ever say. But sometimes, love wasn't enough to overcome the realities of life.

When she returned home, they met again, as they always did. They didn't speak of the future, didn't mention the distance that was slowly growing between them. Instead, they held onto the present, to the love that still existed between them, even as it slipped through their fingers like sand. And in that moment, they prayed for better days, even though they both knew that their prayers might never be answered.

CHAPTER VI

THE WEIGHT OF UNSPOKEN GOODBYES

Arjun sat by the window of his house, staring out at the horizon where the sun had begun to set. The golden light filtered through the sheer curtains, casting long shadows on the floor. In a few hours, he would be on a plane, leaving behind the town that had shaped him, the people who had loved him, and, most painfully, Meera. He had packed his bags days ago, methodically folding clothes and placing his books between layers of fabric. But his heart felt heavy, burdened by a choice he hadn't wanted to make. He had wanted to stay for Meera, had almost made the decision to abandon his dream of studying architecture abroad. He could have built something here, he told himself, something beautiful and meaningful—something that could have included her.

But deep down, Arjun knew that staying would have been a betrayal of everything he had worked for, everything that he had dreamed of since he was a boy. Architecture was more than a career to him; it was a way of seeing the world, of creating spaces that had never existed before. It was his calling, and he knew he had to follow it, even if it meant leaving behind the person he loved most. As much as he loved Meera, he couldn't shake the feeling that staying would have confined her, too. He had seen the way her family clung to her, how they shaped her life with their expectations. If he stayed, would she be able to be herself, or would she feel the same burden of duty that kept her bound to them? He had no answer, only the gnawing feeling that their love, as beautiful as it was, could not bloom in the confines of their circumstances.

Arjun sighed and ran a hand through his hair, closing his eyes as memories of their time together washed over him—their chance meeting at the book fair, the stolen moments in the café, the letters they exchanged, and the long conversations that had filled the quiet spaces between them. Their love had been pure and innocent, a connection that had required nothing but presence and sincerity. Yet now, it felt like the weight of the world had settled on his shoulders, forcing him to make decisions that neither of them had wanted to face.

He wasn't ready to say goodbye, not to her. But life had a way of pulling people apart, even when they tried to hold on with everything they had. In the end, he knew it wasn't just about love; it was about the future—hers, his, and the dreams they both carried.

Across town, Meera stood in her room, the sounds of her family drifting through the house. Her mother's voice mingled with the clattering of pots and pans in the kitchen, while her father's deep, authoritative tone echoed from the living room. It was a familiar scene, one that had played out for as long as she could remember, yet tonight it felt different. She had just come from meeting Arjun, and though their time together had been filled with laughter and warmth, a sense of finality lingered in her heart. She hadn't told him everything—about the conversations she had overheard in the days leading up to his departure, the hushed voices of her family talking about her future, about marriage, about settling down with someone "suitable." Someone who wouldn't challenge the boundaries they had drawn around her life.

Meera had listened in silence, her heart sinking as she realized the implications of what they were saying. Her family's vision for her life didn't include Arjun. They didn't know about him, not really, but even if they did, it wouldn't matter. To them, love was something that came after duty—after responsibility had been fulfilled. And in their eyes, Arjun didn't fit into the picture they had carefully constructed for her. But Meera didn't want to lose him. Their love was different—it wasn't bound by the rules of society or the expectations of her family. It was something pure, something that had blossomed in the quiet moments they shared, in the letters they exchanged, in the way they understood each other without needing to speak. She loved him deeply, and she knew he loved her, too.

Yet, as much as she wanted to hold on to him, she knew that their paths were diverging. He was leaving for a future filled with possibility, a future she couldn't follow. Her responsibilities kept her anchored here, and she couldn't abandon them, no matter how much she wished she could. There were moments when Meera had thought about running away with Arjun, of leaving everything behind and building a life together. But those thoughts had always been fleeting, swept away by the reality of her situation. She couldn't leave her family; they needed her, and that need was stronger than her desire to escape.

Still, she couldn't bring herself to tell Arjun the full truth. Instead, she had met him with a smile, shared their usual laughter, and avoided the weighty conversation they both knew was coming. She didn't want to ruin the time they had left. She wanted to hold on to the magic of their love for as long as possible, even if it meant living in denial of what was coming next. As she lay down in her bed that night, Meera clutched a letter Arjun had written to her earlier that week. His words were filled with hope, with dreams of a future where they could be together, where they could build a life on their own terms. She wished she could believe in that future, but the voices of her family echoed in her mind, reminding her that some dreams were too far out of reach.

Tears filled her eyes as she thought about the days to come. She would miss him terribly, but she knew she had to let him go. Their love, as beautiful as it was, couldn't survive the reality of their lives. But that didn't mean it wasn't real. It was, and it always would be, a love that transcended time and distance. For now, they would continue as they had been—exchanging letters, meeting when they could, and holding on to the connection that had brought them together in the first place. But the looming separation hung over them like a shadow, unspoken yet undeniable.

And so, with hearts heavy but full of love, they would walk their diverging paths, knowing that no matter where life took them, a part of each other would always remain.

CHAPTER VII

THE PROMISE OF LIFE

The coffee shop was quiet, the soft clinking of cups and the murmur of conversations blending into the background as Arjun and Meera sat across from each other. Outside, the city moved on, unaware of the weight of the moment unfolding inside this small corner café, the place that had been their sanctuary for so long. They had met here countless times, exchanging letters, sharing their hopes, and basking in the quiet comfort of each other's company. But today felt different. Today was their last meeting—perhaps forever.

Arjun looked at Meera, taking in every detail of her face, memorizing the curve of her smile, the way her eyes lit up when she laughed, and the subtle way she tilted her head when she was lost in thought. He had seen that look many times, but today it felt precious, fleeting. He reached across the table, his hand finding hers. "I don't know how we got here, Meera," he said softly, his voice thick with emotion. "It feels like just yesterday we met at that book fair. I was so sure of everything then, and now... now it's all so unclear."

Meera smiled, though her eyes betrayed the sadness she had been trying to hide. "Life has a way of changing things, doesn't it?" she replied, her fingers gently intertwining with his. "I never imagined we'd be sitting here, saying goodbye. But I guess that's what happens when you don't have control over everything."

There was a long pause as they both let the words settle. Arjun had always been the more ambitious one, always looking forward, always planning for the future. Meera, on the other hand, had been content with the present, always finding beauty in the simplicity of their time together. But now, their paths were diverging in ways neither of them could have predicted.

"I've been thinking a lot about us," Arjun said finally, his gaze fixed on the cup of coffee in front of him. "About how we're... made for each other. It's strange, isn't it? We fit so perfectly, but life is pulling us in different directions. I don't want to go, Meera. I don't want to leave you behind."

Meera squeezed his hand gently, her heart aching at the truth of his words. She had known for a while now that this day was coming, that Arjun would be leaving for his studies abroad, and that her future was still uncertain. Her family had their expectations, and she had her responsibilities. She couldn't follow him, no matter how much she wanted to.

"I don't want you to go either," she whispered, her voice barely audible. "But we both knew this day would come, didn't we? You have your dreams, Arjun. And I... I have mine, too, even if they're not as clear as yours."

Arjun looked up at her then, his eyes searching hers for something—an answer, a solution, anything that would make this easier. But there was nothing to be found. They were both mature enough to understand that love, no matter how deep and true, didn't always guarantee a shared future.

"I've been asking myself," he continued, "if we should stay in touch after I leave. Letters, emails... I don't know if that's going to be enough, Meera. What if they stop reaching you? What if one day we just... stop writing? I don't want to lose you, not like that."

Meera's heart clenched at the thought. The idea of drifting apart slowly, of their connection fading into silence, was unbearable. But she knew Arjun was right. Once he was gone, once they were both absorbed in their separate lives, staying in touch would be difficult, if not impossible. The world was vast, and they would both be swept up in its currents.

"I've thought about that too," Meera admitted, her voice breaking slightly. "I don't want to lose what we have. I don't want to wake up one day and realize that we've become strangers. But I also don't want to hold you back, Arjun. You have so much ahead of you, so much potential. You can't be weighed down by me, by us."

Arjun shook his head, his grip tightening on her hand. "You could never weigh me down, Meera. You're the reason I've become who I am. You've given me so much—more than you know."

They sat in silence for a moment, both of them grappling with the reality of the situation. They had been so sure of their love, so sure that it could withstand anything. But now, faced with the uncertainty of the future, they weren't so sure anymore. They had no idea what lay ahead, no way of knowing if their paths would ever cross again.

"Maybe..." Meera began hesitantly, "maybe we don't need to decide anything right now. Maybe we just... let life happen. But..." She paused, her heart pounding as an idea began to take shape in her mind. "What if we make a pact? A promise to each other."

Arjun frowned slightly, intrigued. "A *pact*?"

Meera nodded, her voice growing stronger. "Yes. A pact. No matter what happens, no matter where life takes us, let's promise to meet here—exactly forty years from now. Right here, in this café."

Arjun's eyes widened in surprise. "Forty years? Meera, that's..."

"I know it's a long time," she said quickly, "but think about it. In forty years, we'll both have lived our lives. We'll have gone through everything life has to offer—joy, pain, love, loss. And if we're still meant to be together, if we're still the same people who fell in love all those years ago, then we'll meet again. And we'll know."

Arjun stared at her, his heart swelling with a mixture of love and sadness. It was a beautiful idea—one that spoke to the depth of their connection and the hope that, even after all the years and the miles, they would still find their way back to each other.

"But what if we don't make it?" he asked softly. "What if we don't meet again?"

Meera smiled, a tear slipping down her cheek. "Then we'll know that life had other plans for us. But at least we'll have honored what we had. We'll have given each other the chance to live fully, without holding on to something that might not be possible. And if we do meet again... then maybe it means we were always meant to be."

Arjun felt a lump in his throat as he processed her words. It was both heartbreaking and hopeful, a testament to the love they had shared and the respect they had for each other's futures. He could see the wisdom in it, even if it pained him to think about the years they would spend apart.

"Okay," he said finally, his voice thick with emotion. "Let's make the pact."

They both stood up, and Arjun pulled her into his arms, holding her tightly as if trying to memorize the feel of her against him. Meera buried her face in his chest, inhaling the familiar scent of him, knowing that this was the last time they would be together like this for a long time—if ever again.

"I'll see you here," she whispered, her voice muffled against his shirt. "Forty years from today. No matter what."

Arjun nodded, though the words felt like a promise too far into the future to truly comprehend. "I'll be here," he whispered back. "I'll always be here for you, Meera."

They pulled apart, their hands lingering for just a moment longer before finally letting go. Neither of them said another word as they left the café, walking in opposite directions, their hearts heavy with the weight of their love and the uncertainty of what was to come. But as they walked away, both of them held on to the hope that, forty years from now, they would meet again and discover whether their love had truly endured the test of time.

PART II

ECHOES OF SILENCE

CHAPTER VIII

BLUEPRINTS OF THE HEART

Arjun stared at the towering skyline outside his window, the gleaming glass buildings reflecting the late afternoon sun. It was a city brimming with life, energy, and ambition—exactly what he had once longed for. But now, standing here miles away from everything familiar, all he felt was a sense of emptiness. The dream he had worked so hard to realize suddenly felt incomplete. He turned back to his desk, where a half-finished sketch of a building lay in front of him. His professors praised his modern designs, lauding his talent for combining sleek lines with innovative functionality. But every time Arjun picked up his pencil, he found himself drawn to something else entirely—something softer, more timeless. He couldn't shake the idea of creating spaces that felt permanent, like a home you never wanted to leave. Like a love that stood the test of time. His thoughts wandered back to Meera, as they often did, and his hand instinctively reached for the stack of letters tucked into his notebook. He had carried them with him, a secret lifeline to the world he had left behind. Gently, he unfolded the one on top, the delicate handwriting instantly transporting him back to the moments they had shared.

"Dear Arjun," the letter began, "I don't know what the future holds, but I hope that wherever you are, you're happy. I hope that you're creating something beautiful, something that lasts. Because that's who you are—someone who builds not just with bricks and stone, but with his heart."

Arjun clenched the paper in his hand, his chest tightening as he reread her words. Meera always had a way of seeing through him, of understanding the unspoken thoughts that lingered just beneath the surface. He had told himself that leaving was the right choice, that pursuing his dreams was what he needed to do. But now, he wasn't so sure. Every sketch, every design he created seemed to lead him back to her, to the idea of home. Not just any home—a home that felt like her. He closed his eyes and let his mind drift, imagining her sitting across from him at the café, her soft smile lighting up her face as she talked about the latest book she was reading. He could hear her laugh, the way it filled the air with warmth and comfort. There was a simplicity to their love, a purity that had been effortless. And yet, it was the very thing he had chosen to leave behind in search of something more.

But what was more? Arjun couldn't help but question. He had always believed that success, fame, and recognition were what mattered, that his talent and ambition would take him places he could only dream of. And yet, now that he was here, surrounded by the opportunity and promise of a bright future, it all felt hollow.

The apartment he lived in was beautiful, no doubt—a minimalist haven with high ceilings and expansive views. But it felt cold, empty, devoid of life. It wasn't a place where love thrived, where memories were made. It wasn't home.

And it wasn't Meera.

He looked at the sketches scattered across his desk—buildings, structures, ideas that all felt detached, like they belonged to someone else. They were modern, innovative, but they lacked soul. They lacked the heart that had once fueled his passion for architecture. He had always been drawn to spaces that told stories, places that held memories within their walls. Now, all he could think about was how to create something timeless—something that would stand the test of time, like his love for her.

Arjun sighed, leaning back in his chair as he rubbed his temples. He hadn't made any new friends since arriving. Sure, there were colleagues, people he met in classes or at work, but he had been reluctant to open up, to let anyone in. The idea of starting over, of meeting someone new, felt impossible. His heart was still in that small café, in the city he had left behind, with the woman he couldn't stop thinking about. It wasn't that he didn't try. He had told himself that moving on was the right thing to do, that time would heal the longing in his chest. But every time he tried to focus on something else, something pulled him back. Maybe it was the pact they had made—the promise to meet again in forty years. Maybe it was the memory of her laugh, the way her eyes lit up when she talked about the future, even though they both knew it was uncertain.

He pulled out another letter from the stack, this one a little more worn from being read so many times. A letter full of hope and encouragement. "We're on different paths, Arjun," it said, "but that doesn't mean we've lost each other. We're still connected, even if we're far apart. And maybe, one day, our paths will cross again."

Arjun felt a lump form in his throat. He wanted to believe her, to believe that time and distance wouldn't change what they had. But part of him was scared—scared that life would take them too far from each other, that they would become different people, shaped by their separate experiences. And yet, he couldn't let go. He couldn't stop thinking about her, about the life they might have had if things had been different. He wondered if she thought about him, too—if she held onto their letters the way he did, if she still dreamed of that day when they would meet again in the café, older but still full of the love that had once defined them.

Arjun folded the letters carefully, placing them back in his notebook. He knew he couldn't live in the past, but he also knew that Meera had become a part of him, woven into the very fabric of who he was. His designs, though modern, were inspired by the timelessness of old-school love stories—the kind that endured, that left a mark on your soul. As he picked up his pencil to finish the sketch in front of him, Arjun found himself drawing not just a building, but a home. A place filled with warmth, with love, with memories. A place where two people could sit together, sharing a moment that would last a lifetime.

He drew, not for his professors or his future clients, but for Meera—for the love that continued to inspire him, even from across the distance.

CHAPTER IX

BETWEEN THE LINES

Meera sat by the window of her small apartment, the golden afternoon light filtering through the curtains as she gazed absentmindedly at the old oak tree outside. Her notebooks were scattered across the table, filled with pages of thoughts, musings, and poetry. Though she had moved to pursue her passion for literature, her heart often drifted to thoughts of Arjun. It wasn't a conscious decision to think of him— it simply happened. As she immersed herself in romantic poetry and the old classics, his presence seemed to echo in the words she read and the stories she wrote. She had thrown herself into her studies, delving into the works of Keats, Shelley, and Eliot. The beauty of their language, the way they captured longing and loss, resonated deeply with her. It was as though the words on the page were speaking her unspoken thoughts, her hidden emotions. The more she read, the more she found herself unconsciously mirroring Arjun's sentimentality, her love for literature becoming a vessel for her love for him.

Meera's days were spent in libraries, her evenings in cafés, where she engaged in literary discussions with fellow students and professors. She had become a literature student not just in the academic sense, but in the very essence of who she was. Every line of poetry she read, every novel she devoured, seemed to pull her further into a world where Arjun still existed in the background. She remembered their discussions, the long conversations about life, love, and the future. How Arjun would talk about architecture with the same passion she felt for literature. It was as though their dreams, though different in form, were connected by a shared sense of beauty, of wanting to create something timeless. Meera often found herself thinking about the homes he had talked about building, how they weren't just structures but spaces meant to hold memories, to capture love.

Even in her writing, she found herself drawing parallels between her stories and the memories she held of him. There were characters in her stories who longed for love but were bound by circumstances, who found solace in letters and fleeting moments. It was as though she couldn't help but write about what she felt deep down—this unspoken connection that lingered, even as they lived separate lives. Yet, despite this undercurrent of longing, Meera had become aloof from the world around her. She attended classes, engaged in discussions, and participated in all the activities expected of her. But there was a part of her that remained distant, as if she were standing on the outside looking in. She had become adept at hiding her feelings, at keeping the world at arm's length.

Her professors often praised her for her insight into the works they studied, noting how deeply she seemed to understand the themes of love, loss, and separation. They didn't know that her understanding came not just from the books she read, but from the life she had lived. It was as though the pain of being apart from Arjun had heightened her sensitivity to the emotions expressed in the literature she loved. In her quiet moments, when she wasn't surrounded by the buzz of university life, Meera would write. Her journal had become a place where she poured out her thoughts, her reflections on love, life, and the path she had chosen. She didn't write about Arjun directly—there were no mentions of his name or their time together. But the essence of him was in every word, in every line.

She often wondered if he thought about her too. If, in the midst of his architectural studies, he found himself sketching buildings that reminded him of the café they had spent so much time in, or the moments they had shared. She imagined him walking through bustling streets, seeing something—a window, a doorframe, a bridge—that made him think of her.

There was an unspoken connection between them, one that neither distance nor time could erase. It was as though they were both walking along separate paths, but those paths were somehow parallel, running alongside each other, never fully crossing but always close enough to feel the other's presence. Meera clutched the pen in her hand, the ink flowing effortlessly onto the page as she wrote a poem that had been forming in her mind. It was about two souls, separated by circumstance but forever tied by a thread of love. They walked through life, never quite meeting, but always feeling the other's presence in the spaces they passed through. It was a reflection of her own life, of the quiet love she still carried for Arjun.

She had never stopped loving him, not truly. But she had come to accept that life had different plans for them. It was a hard truth, one that had taken her time to come to terms with. But as the months passed, she found comfort in the idea that love didn't always have to follow a conventional path. She knew that what they had was special, that it would always be a part of her, even if they never saw each other again.

And yet, despite this acceptance, there was still a small part of her that clung to the hope of their pact— the promise to meet again in forty years. It was a dream, perhaps a foolish one, but it gave her something to hold onto. It was a testament to the love they had shared, a love that had never needed labels or boundaries. Meera looked down at the poem she had just written, her heart full of both longing and peace. She knew that their paths, though separate, were still intertwined in some way. And maybe, just maybe, one day those paths would cross again. Until then, she would continue to write, to read, to find solace in the words that had always brought her comfort. Because in the end, that was what connected them—two souls, bound by a love that transcended time and space.

CHAPTER X

THE SPACE BETWEEN

Arjun stood by the window of his office, looking out at the cityscape. It was a skyline of his own making—a testament to his success as an architect. The buildings he had designed were known for their modernity, but if one looked closely enough, there were hidden elements that told a different story. Small arches, intricate carvings, and timeless courtyards that whispered of old-school love stories and spaces meant to last forever.

But today, as he looked out at those buildings, they felt cold to him. He was surrounded by the life he had dreamed of, yet something was missing. It wasn't the buildings or the accolades that weighed on him. It was the absence of Meera.

It had been two years since they last connected.

Two years since that final goodbye in the café, where they had made a pact to meet again in forty years. He still held on to that promise, but the passing time had created a silence that was hard to ignore. They hadn't exchanged letters or emails, as they had once so frequently done. Life had carried them in different directions, and Arjun couldn't help but wonder if she had forgotten about him, or if she too was simply lost in her own world, just as he was in his. For a long time, Arjun had buried himself in his work. It was easier that way—focusing on designs, deadlines, and clients. It distracted him from the longing, from the aching void that Meera had left behind. His creativity was fueled by the emotions he never spoke about. Every project he worked on seemed to reflect some part of their story, whether it was a bench under an old oak tree or a hidden courtyard that felt like an escape from the world.

But his personal life had become a wasteland. He had become ruthless in his pursuit of success, absorbed in his career to the point where he barely noticed the people around him. There had been women who had shown interest in him, but Arjun had never entertained the idea of letting someone new into his heart. How could he, when Meera still occupied every corner of it?

There was one woman, however, who had persisted. She was too sweet, too kind, and far too good for him—at least, that's how Arjun saw it. Her name was Ria, and she had a way of making him laugh, even when he didn't want to. She had been trying, in her own gentle way, to press into his life, to make it better. She brought him coffee in the mornings, checked in on him when he worked late into the night, and always seemed to know when he needed a moment of peace.

But Arjun kept his distance. He couldn't let her in.

One night, as they sat together after a long day at work, she had looked at him with those soft, hopeful eyes and said, "You know, Arjun, you could be my passion."

He had smiled, but there was sadness behind it. "I could be your passion, Ria. But I can't be your lover."

She didn't understand, of course. How could she? He hadn't told her about Meera, about the woman who still haunted his every thought. Ria deserved someone who could give her all the love she needed, but Arjun couldn't be that person. His heart was still tangled up in a love that had no resolution, in a promise that had been made on a whim, but one he still believed in.

One evening, as Arjun sat in his office, exhausted from the weight of his own life, he found himself browsing through an online literary magazine. It had become a habit for him—reading poetry and stories, hoping to find traces of Meera in the words. He had always admired her writing, and though she hadn't published much back when they were together, he sometimes wondered if she had started again. Maybe, just maybe, he would stumble upon her words and feel that connection again. He scrolled through the latest issue, skimming through poems and short stories, but nothing caught his attention. Not until he came across a quote in a piece about love and memory. The words seemed to leap off the screen, piercing through the haze that had clouded his heart for so long.

"Loving someone is not always about being together. Sometimes, it's about honoring their memory by becoming the person they always believed you could be."

Arjun stared at the quote, his breath catching in his

throat. There was something about those words that felt familiar, something that stirred deep within him. It wasn't just the sentiment—it was the voice behind it. He read the author's name at the bottom of the article, but it didn't register. It wasn't Meera's name. But that didn't matter. He knew, in his heart, that these words had come from her. Suddenly, it all made sense. The reason why he had been unable to let go, why he had kept searching for her even after two years of silence. He had been clinging to the idea that their love was unfinished, that they needed to be together to give it meaning. But that wasn't true. Their love was timeless, and it didn't need to be confined by time or space. It was something greater, something that had shaped him in ways he hadn't even realized.

Arjun sat back in his chair, closing his eyes as the weight of the past two years began to lift. He had been so absorbed in his life, in his work, that he had forgotten the most important lesson Meera had ever taught him—that love wasn't about possession or proximity. It was about growth. It was about honoring the person you loved by becoming the best version of yourself, even if you couldn't be with them. He thought about the life he had built, the buildings he had designed, the people he had shut out. He realized now that he had been doing it all wrong. He had been trying to forget, trying to move on by burying himself in his work. But that wasn't what Meera would have wanted. She would have wanted him to live fully, to embrace the world with the same passion they had shared together.

The next morning, Arjun woke up feeling lighter than he had in years. He still missed Meera, still longed for her in ways he couldn't fully articulate. But he knew now that he didn't need to hold onto that longing anymore. He could carry her with him, not as a weight, but as a source of inspiration. Her memory, her love, would be the foundation on which he built the rest of his life. As he left his office that day, Ria smiled at him from across the room. For the first time, he smiled back without the shadow of hesitation. He wasn't ready to open his heart to her, not yet. But maybe, in time, he would be.

For now, he had Meera's words to guide him, and that was enough.

CHAPTER XI

The Weight of Unspoken Things

With her fingers gliding over the pages of an old poetry book she'd found in a second-hand shop, Meera sat. The smell of the aged paper, the faded ink, and the soft, worn corners reminded her of a time when life seemed simpler—when love was something pure and untouched, rather than weighed down by the complexities of adulthood. She closed her eyes for a moment, letting herself drift back to memories of Arjun, their days together filled with unspoken promises and shared silences. But that time felt far away now, like a distant echo from another life. It had been over two years since they had last spoken. Their lives had diverged, and Meera had accepted it, at least on the surface. She had immersed herself in her studies, becoming a literature student just as she had always dreamed. Romantic poetry and classic novels became her sanctuary, her refuge from the weight of family expectations and societal pressures. In every poem she read, every line she wrote, there was a trace of Arjun— his love for architecture, his passion for creating spaces that told stories. Though they were worlds apart, she could still feel his presence in her life, even if it was only through the echoes of their shared past.

Meera had become an accomplished writer. Her essays and articles were published in literary magazines, and she often found herself leading discussions on romantic poetry, much to the admiration of her peers. She wrote with a maturity that surprised even her—her words seemed to carry the weight of her experiences, of the love she had known and the life she had chosen to live. Her thoughts spilled onto the pages of her journals, filled with reflections on love, loss, and the quiet beauty of moments that are never meant to last.

Yet, despite her outward success, Meera still found herself seeking traces of Arjun. Every now and then, she would come across an architecture journal and leaf through its pages, her heart racing as she searched for his name, for some sign that he was doing well. She never found him, but the act of searching gave her a strange sense of comfort, as though looking for him in those pages was a way of keeping him close. It wasn't that she hadn't moved on; she had accepted their separation with a quiet resignation. But some part of her still longed for a connection, a reminder that what they had shared had been real. As she stared out the window, watching the sun dip below the horizon, Meera felt the familiar weight of her family's expectations pressing down on her. The talk of marriage had become more insistent over the past few months, her parents dropping subtle hints and not-so-subtle suggestions that it was time for her to settle down. They had even introduced her to a few potential suitors, men who were kind and successful, but none of them stirred her heart the way Arjun had. She had smiled politely, nodded in all the right places, but her heart remained untouched, her mind wandering back to the boy who had once made her believe in a love that transcended time and distance.

Her family, of course, didn't understand. They saw her as a dutiful daughter, someone who had done well academically and was now expected to fulfill her role as a wife and mother. Meera had tried to explain, in the gentlest way possible, that she wasn't ready, that she needed more time. But time, as they reminded her, was not on her side. The pressure was mounting, and she knew that soon, she would have to make a decision. But how could she? How could she commit to someone else when her heart still carried the memory of Arjun? She had tried to bury those feelings, to convince herself that they were nothing more than remnants of a past that could never be reclaimed. But every time she sat down to write, every time she read a passage from one of her favorite books, she felt his presence there with her. It wasn't that she was waiting for him—she knew that their lives had taken different paths, and she had made peace with that. But the love they had shared had shaped her in ways she couldn't fully explain. It had become a part of who she was, woven into the fabric of her being.

Meera sighed, her thoughts drifting back to the last time she had seen him. They had stood in that coffee shop, their hands brushing against each other as they made a pact—a promise to meet again, forty years from now, in that very place. It had been a romantic gesture, one born out of love and hope, but also out of a deep understanding that their lives were heading in different directions. They had sworn to honor each other's memory, to move forward in life without bitterness or regret. And yet, as much as she had tried to do just that, there were moments when she felt like she was still standing in that coffee shop, waiting for him to turn around and come back to her.

Her phone buzzed, pulling her out of her reverie. It was her mother, calling to remind her about an upcoming family gathering. Meera closed her eyes, steeling herself for yet another round of questions about her future. She knew what was coming—the pointed glances, the subtle comments about her being too focused on her studies, about how it was time for her to think about marriage and starting a family. She would smile, nod, and give the same answers she always did. But inside, she felt the weight of their expectations growing heavier with each passing day. She stood up and walked over to her bookshelf, her fingers grazing the spines of her favorite books. These were her companions, her escape from the world that demanded so much from her. She pulled out a volume of romantic poetry and opened it to a page she had marked years ago. The words leapt off the page, speaking to her in a way that no conversation ever could:

"Love is not about possession, but about the freedom to let the heart wander, to find joy in the memory of what once was."

Meera smiled softly to herself. It was a lesson she had learned from Arjun, from the love they had shared.

Their love had never been about possession or control; it had been about freedom—freedom to grow, to change, to follow their own paths while still carrying the memory of each other. It wasn't an easy lesson to learn, but it had shaped her in ways she hadn't expected. She knew that she would always carry a part of Arjun with her, just as he would carry a part of her. And maybe that was enough.

She placed the book back on the shelf and glanced at her desk, where a stack of papers awaited her attention. Her latest project, a collection of essays on love and loss, was nearly complete. It was her way of processing the emotions she had carried with her for so long, of making sense of the love that had shaped her life. She sat down and picked up her pen, her mind drifting back to Arjun as she began to write. In her heart, she knew that their paths had diverged. But in her writing, in the words that flowed from her pen, she found a connection that transcended time and distance. And though she didn't know what the future held, she knew one thing for certain: the love they had shared would always be a part of her, woven into the fabric of her words, her thoughts, and her life.

CHAPTER XII

FRAGMENTS OF WHAT WAS

Arjun sat in his living room, the soft glow of the evening sun filtering through the large glass windows, casting long shadows on the wooden floor. The architectural lines of the space were clean, modern, and sleek—his signature style. It was a reflection of how far he had come in his career. Each curve, every angle, had a purpose, designed with precision. But even in this moment of apparent accomplishment, a heaviness clung to him, a kind of nostalgia that gnawed at the edges of his heart. Ria's voice pulled him from his thoughts. She was in the kitchen, humming a soft tune as she prepared tea. They had been together for a year now, slowly building a relationship that was both tender and familiar. Ria was everything one could wish for—kind, warm, with a gentle smile that could ease the harshest of days. She loved him deeply, and in return, Arjun found himself slowly opening to the idea of a settled life with her. But despite the growing affection he felt for her, there was a part of him that remained distant, locked away in a corner of his heart where Meera still lived.

Ria placed a cup of tea in front of him and sat beside him on the couch. She looked at him with those soft, understanding eyes, the kind that asked no questions but somehow knew all the answers. He smiled at her, a grateful, genuine smile, and sipped the tea, letting its warmth settle inside him.

"You've been quiet lately," she said gently, reaching out to hold his hand. "Is everything alright?"

Arjun hesitated for a moment, his mind flickering back to Meera. It had been years since they last spoke, and yet, her memory had never left him. There were days when he would catch himself thinking about her, wondering how she was, where she was, and if she had moved on like he had. He knew it was irrational to hold on to a love that had faded into the past, yet here he was, still haunted by her absence.

"I'm fine," he replied, squeezing Ria's hand gently. "Just... thinking about the future, I suppose."

Ria smiled, her eyes lighting up at his words. She had been patient with him, never pushing too hard, always giving him the space to navigate his emotions at his own pace. And now, it seemed, he was finally moving toward the life they had envisioned together— a life of stability, marriage, perhaps even a family. It was a life Arjun had always imagined for himself, but somehow, in every vision, there had always been Meera. Later that evening, after Ria had fallen asleep, Arjun sat in his study, the faint light of a desk lamp illuminating the room. He reached for the book that had become his refuge in these moments of quiet reflection—an old collection of poetry, one of Meera's favorites. Flipping through the pages, his eyes fell on a quote she had once shared with him, one that had stayed with him ever since:

"Love does not bind; it frees us to become the best versions of ourselves."

The words struck him differently now. Perhaps it was because, for the first time, he was beginning to let go. He had loved Meera deeply, but that love had always been unspoken, undefined. Now, with Ria in his life, he was starting to understand that loving someone didn't always mean being with them. Sometimes, love meant letting go, allowing the other person to grow, to live their own life. He sighed and closed the book, feeling a sense of peace wash over him. Ria deserved all of him, and slowly, he was learning to give her that.

On the other side of the world, Meera sat by her desk, staring out at the evening sky. The weight of her family's expectations pressed down on her, as it had been for the past few months. The conversations at home had become more pointed, the pressure to marry growing stronger with each passing day. Her parents had introduced her to several men, each of them polite, well-mannered, and suitable. But none of them stirred her heart.

Her mind drifted to Arjun. She hadn't heard from him, but the memories of their time together remained vivid. She often found herself wondering if he had moved on, if he had found someone to share his life with. The thought both comforted and saddened her. She wanted him to be happy, of course, but some part of her still longed for the life they had once imagined—a life where they would have been together, sharing their love for literature and architecture, building a future together. Meera sighed and reached for the notebook that sat open on her desk. It was filled with her writings—poems, essays, reflections on love and loss. She had become a well-regarded writer, her words resonating with readers who saw themselves in her stories of unrequited love and longing. But even as she poured her heart onto the page, there was a part of her that remained untouched, hidden away from the world. It was the part of her that still belonged to Arjun.

Her parents knocked on the door, interrupting her thoughts. They entered, their faces filled with concern and a touch of impatience. Her mother sat down beside her, taking her hand.

"Meera, we've found someone," her mother said gently. "He's a good man, from a good family. It's time for you to think about your future, about settling down."

Meera nodded, her throat tightening. She knew what was expected of her. She was a dutiful daughter, after all, and her parents had always been supportive of her ambitions. But the thought of marrying someone she didn't love, someone who wasn't Arjun, felt like a betrayal of everything she held dear.

"I understand, Ma," she whispered. "I just need some time."

Her mother smiled softly, brushing a strand of hair away from Meera's face. "We don't want to pressure you, beta. We just want you to be happy."

After her parents left, Meera sat in silence, her heart heavy with the weight of their expectations. She had always been a good daughter, doing what was asked of her without complaint. But now, as she stood on the precipice of a life she hadn't chosen, she felt lost. How could she marry someone else when her heart still belonged to Arjun?

She glanced at the stack of architecture magazines on her desk. Every now and then, she would pick one up, flipping through the pages in search of Arjun's name. She had never found him, but the act of searching gave her a strange sense of comfort, as though it was her way of keeping him close. But now, as the pressure to marry grew, she knew that she couldn't keep holding on to the past. She had to move forward, even if it meant letting go of the love she had carried with her for so long. That night, as she lay in bed, Meera's thoughts drifted back to the last time she had seen Arjun. They had made a pact to meet again, forty years from now, in that same coffee shop where they had shared so many moments together. It had been a romantic gesture, a way of keeping their love alive even as they moved forward with their lives. But now, as she faced the reality of her future, Meera wondered if they would ever meet again.

Would Arjun remember their pact? Or had he already moved on, building a life with someone else?

The thought brought a pang of sadness, but also a sense of acceptance. Meera knew that she couldn't hold on to the past forever. She had to live her life, to honor the love she had shared with Arjun by moving forward and finding happiness in the present. And perhaps, one day, their paths would cross again. But for now, she would let go, trusting that the love they had shared would remain a part of her, even as she built a new life.

As the months passed, both Arjun and Meera found

themselves moving toward their respective futures. Arjun, with Ria by his side, began to imagine a life of stability, of marriage and family. And though the memory of Meera still lingered, he found peace in the knowledge that their love had shaped him, had made him the man he was today. He would always carry her with him, but he was ready to give his heart fully to Ria. Meera, too, began to accept her path. She allowed herself to be open to the idea of marriage, though her heart still held a quiet space for Arjun. She had learned to love without possession, to honor the memory of what they had shared by living fully in the present. And though she didn't know what the future held, she knew one thing for certain: the love they had shared would always be a part of her, woven into the fabric of her life, no matter where her journey took her. And so, they moved forward, each on their own path, bound by the love they had once known, but free to live their own lives. Their story was not one of endings, but of beginnings—of growth, of change, and of the quiet, enduring love that would stay with them always, even as they followed the paths life had laid before them.

CHAPTER XIII

THE QUIET CONTINUUM

Time had passed, and with it, the lives of Arjun and Meera had evolved into something that resembled what most would call "moving on." They had both married, found companionship in their partners, and built lives filled with the ordinary rhythm of days that every now and then pulsed with small joys, challenges, and the mundane obligations of adulthood. But underneath this seemingly perfect surface, there was a lingering presence of something else, something that neither could name, but both felt with quiet intensity. Arjun had become an internationally recognized architect. His works graced the pages of design magazines, his name now whispered in elite circles of creativity and vision. Yet, despite his outward success, there was a subtle melancholy that had settled into the lines of his face, a weight he carried in his heart. He was married to Ria, a kind and wonderful woman who had become the steady presence in his life. Ria had supported him through the ups and downs of his career, had been his rock when he'd felt overwhelmed by the pressures of his industry. She was good for him, and in his own way, Arjun loved her.

But there were moments—quiet, fleeting moments—when Arjun would find himself staring out of the large, pristine windows of his studio, watching the world outside but seeing nothing, lost in the echo of a past that had never quite left him. He would run his fingers over the spines of old architectural sketches and journals, and sometimes, a memory of Meera would surface with a pang so sharp it would take his breath away. In those moments, Arjun would close his eyes, and in the darkness, he could still see her smile, still hear her voice. He had tried to bury it, had tried to lock it away, but love has a way of seeping through the cracks, no matter how much time had passed. It was on one of those days, while flipping through an architecture journal, that something caught his eye—a quote nestled within an article on literature and its influence on modern design. The words felt familiar, a cadence he had not heard in years. It was Meera's voice, unmistakable, as though it had been plucked from the very essence of her soul and placed within those lines. He stared at the page, heart hammering in his chest. It was a small excerpt from one of her books, a piece he had never read before. Though her name wasn't mentioned directly in the article, the unmistakable style, the delicate, poignant reflection of love and life, resonated so deeply with him that he knew it could only have come from her.

He swallowed hard, his hands trembling as he traced the words on the page. She was still out there, still writing, still pouring her heart into the world through her stories. And though they hadn't spoken in years, though he was married to someone else now, in that moment, he felt connected to her again in a way that no amount of time or distance could sever. It was as though her words had reached across the years and touched the very core of him, reminding him of what had once been and, perhaps, what could never be.

Meanwhile, across the miles, Meera found herself standing in front of a house, an architectural masterpiece that was unlike anything she had ever seen. She had been invited to a literary gathering held by a well-known writer, and the event was hosted in this house—a house that, for reasons she couldn't quite explain, felt strangely familiar. The clean lines, the open spaces, the way the light moved through the rooms— it all reminded her of something, or rather, someone. As she moved through the space, she felt a strange pull, as though the very walls were speaking to her, whispering a name she hadn't allowed herself to say out loud in years.

Arjun.

Though she had never seen his recent work, something deep inside her recognized this house as his creation. She ran her fingers along the bannister, felt the smooth wood beneath her hand, and for a moment, it was as though she could feel his presence there, as though he were standing right beside her. She closed her eyes, remembering the way he had once spoken about his dreams of designing homes—places that felt timeless, that held the stories of the people who lived in them, places that could be filled with love. Meera was married now, too. Her husband, Vikram, was a gentle and kind man, a professor who shared her love for literature and philosophy. They had built a life together, filled with intellectual conversations and quiet companionship. She cared for him deeply, but there were times when she found herself staring out of the window of their modest apartment, wondering what might have been. She would shake herself from those thoughts, reminding herself that life had given her this path, and she had chosen to walk it with Vikram.

But standing in this house, surrounded by Arjun's design, Meera couldn't shake the feeling that their lives were still intertwined, even after all these years. She had tried to bury her feelings for him, had told herself that they had both moved on. Yet, there were nights when she would wake up in the dark, her heart heavy with a longing she couldn't quite explain. And now, being here, in this house that he had created, it was as though all those buried feelings had risen to the surface, raw and unspoken.

Neither Arjun nor Meera knew that their work had crossed each other's paths in this way, that the house Arjun had designed had become a space where Meera had stood, feeling his presence without knowing it was his. And likewise, Arjun had no idea that the words which had moved him so deeply had come from the very woman he had once loved. As they each continued in their respective lives, they found themselves haunted by these quiet connections, these moments where the past brushed up against the present in ways that neither could fully understand. Arjun would sit with Ria, sipping wine on their porch, but his thoughts would drift back to Meera, to the way she had once spoken about love and literature. He would look at Ria, and though he loved her, there was always a part of him that was elsewhere, that still belonged to someone he hadn't seen in years.

Meera, too, would find herself distracted in the middle of conversations with Vikram, her mind drifting back to the house she had visited, to the way it had made her feel. She knew that it was irrational, that it wasn't fair to her husband to hold on to something that was long gone. But love is not something that can be easily erased, and no matter how much she tried, Arjun remained a part of her, woven into the very fabric of her being. They both knew that they had made choices, that they had moved on with their lives, and yet, there was a quiet understanding between them—an understanding that even though they were no longer together, they would always carry each other with them. It was a love that had transcended time and space, a love that had no need for words or contact. It was simply there, existing in the spaces between their lives, in the architecture of a house, in the lines of a book, in the quiet moments when they were alone with their thoughts.

And so, they continued on their parallel paths, living their lives, loving their partners, and yet, always connected by that invisible thread. They didn't need to speak to each other, didn't need to see each other, because the love they had shared was not bound by the physical world. It lived in the spaces they created, in the work they poured their hearts into, in the silent, unseen moments where their lives brushed up against each other without them even knowing. Time would pass, and they would grow older, but that connection would remain, quietly binding them together even as they moved further apart. They had made a pact once, a promise to meet again, but whether or not they ever did, the truth was that they had never really left each other. They had loved, they had let go, and yet, somehow, they had never truly been apart.

In the end, it wasn't about being together—it was about honoring the love they had shared, in their own quiet, unseen ways. And in that, they had found a kind of peace.

PART III

TIDES OF THE UNSEEN

CHAPTER XIV

The Ruins of Life

Arjun stood by the window, staring blankly at the empty cradle in the corner of the room. It had been weeks since Ria had passed, but the silence of the house still gnawed at him, loud and oppressive. The air felt thick, suffocating. Every breath seemed to carry the weight of what had happened—the loss of his wife, the stillborn child who had never opened his eyes, and the inexplicable void that now consumed his life. Ria had been his anchor, the quiet, steady force who had grounded him when his work threatened to overwhelm him. He hadn't realized how much he had leaned on her, how much she had become part of the architecture of his life until she was gone. The illness had come swiftly and without warning, a mysterious, ruthless force that stripped her away from him piece by piece.

First, it was her strength, then her spirit, and finally, her life. Arjun hadn't been prepared—how could he have been? He had watched helplessly as the woman he had built a life with slipped away from him, and with her, the child they had both anticipated with such hope.

Now, the house felt like a mausoleum, a reminder of what he had lost. He would stand in the nursery sometimes, staring at the untouched blankets and tiny clothes, feeling an ache so deep it threatened to pull him under. He had thrown himself into his work, trying to drown out the pain in blueprints and projects, but even that hadn't provided the escape he needed. His designs had become darker, more somber. Gone were the days when his work reflected the lightness of love and romance, the airy spaces that evoked timeless beauty. Now, his buildings felt like fortresses—cold, imposing, and hollow. In the quiet moments, when the world around him was still, memories of Meera would surface, unbidden. He would see her face in the corners of his mind, hear her laugh in the echoes of the past. The pang of guilt would follow quickly after—how could he think of her now, after everything? How could he long for someone he hadn't seen or spoken to in years, when Ria had been the one beside him all this time? But the truth was, Meera had never really left him. She had always been there, lingering in the recesses of his heart, a quiet presence that refused to fade, no matter how much life had changed.

Arjun began to question everything. The choices he had made, the path he had taken—had it all been wrong? Had he missed out on something deeper, something truer with Meera? He found himself wandering through old memories, replaying moments from the past, wondering what could have been if he had fought harder for her, if he had taken a different path. But there were no answers, only the endless what-ifs that circled his mind like vultures. He would wake up in the middle of the night, heart heavy with the weight of everything he had lost, and in those dark hours, he would think of the pact they had made all those years ago.

Across the city, Meera sat at her desk, staring at the pile of papers in front of her, her mind far away from the words she was supposed to be grading. She had become a professor, just as she had dreamed, teaching literature to students who came to her seeking guidance on words and stories. On the surface, her life appeared full—she was respected in her field, her lectures were well-received, and her colleagues admired her dedication. But there was a hollowness inside her that she couldn't shake, a feeling that something essential was missing. Meera's marriage had become strained over the years. Vikram had been a good husband, thoughtful and kind, but their relationship had grown distant. They no longer shared the same connection they once had. The conversations that had once been so easy now felt strained, and there was a growing tension between them that neither of them could ignore. The pressure from her family to stay in the marriage weighed heavily on her. They had always been traditional, and divorce was not something they could easily accept. But the truth was, Meera felt trapped, torn between the life she had built and the one she still longed for.

Lately, thoughts of Arjun had crept into her mind more frequently. She would see something—a book, a quote, a design—and her heart would tug at the memory of him. She had tried so hard to forget, to bury that part of her life, but it had never really gone away. There were times when she would find herself browsing architecture journals, looking for his name, searching for some trace of him. It was a foolish habit, one she had tried to break, but she couldn't help herself. The idea that he might still be out there, living his life, unaware that she was doing the same, filled her with an aching sense of loss. It had been years since they had spoken, but the pact they had made lingered in the back of her mind. They had promised to meet again after forty years, to see if they had been on the right path, to test the endurance of their love. It had seemed like such a romantic notion at the time, a way to honor what they had shared without holding each other back. But now, in the midst of her own personal crisis, that promise felt like a lifeline, a thread that still connected them, even across all the years and miles that separated them.

For Meera, the pressure to leave her work was growing. Her family wanted her to focus on her marriage, to salvage what was left, but she wasn't sure if there was anything left to save. She loved teaching, loved the escape that literature provided her, but it was becoming harder to ignore the growing sense of dissatisfaction in her life. She had once thought that she could have both—a career she was passionate about and a personal life that fulfilled her. But now, it seemed like she was being asked to choose, and the choice felt impossible. As she sat in her office, surrounded by books and papers, Meera found herself thinking about Arjun again. She wondered where he was, what he was doing. Had he built the life he had dreamed of? Was he happy? Did he ever think of her? The questions swirled in her mind, and she had no answers. She had tried to move on, to focus on the life she had, but the truth was, she had never stopped thinking about him.

The realization hit her hard—she had been waiting, all this time. Waiting for something, for someone. And now, faced with the possibility of leaving behind the one thing that gave her solace—her work—Meera felt more lost than ever. She didn't know if she had made the right choices, didn't know if the life she had built was the one she was meant to live. And in the quiet of her office, she found herself whispering a name she hadn't spoken in years.

Arjun found himself wandering through book fairs, something he hadn't done in years. He had never been much of a reader, but Meera had always loved books, and somehow, being surrounded by them made him feel closer to her. He would walk through the stalls, scanning the covers, his fingers brushing the spines of old volumes, hoping—though he didn't know for what. It was as if he were searching for a ghost, for some sign that she was still out there, that their connection hadn't been entirely severed by time. He would linger in the poetry sections, remembering how she used to recite lines from old romantic poets, her eyes lighting up as she spoke the words. Sometimes, he would pick up a book at random, open it to a page, and read, hoping to find something that would bring him back to her. It was a futile exercise, but he couldn't stop himself. He didn't know if she still thought about him, if she even remembered the pact they had made, but for him, it was as real and present as it had ever been.

One day, as he flipped through a book of essays, his heart nearly stopped. There, on the page in front of him, was a quote that struck him with such force that he had to sit down. It was one of Meera's. It was her voice, her way of seeing the world, and in that moment, it felt as though she were speaking directly to him, across all the years and distance. The quote was about love and memory, about how we carry the people we love with us, even when they are no longer by our side. It was beautiful, and it broke him.

Arjun and Meera were both at crossroads, their lives filled with the weight of unspoken words and unfulfilled promises. They had moved on, built lives with other people, but the connection they had shared had never truly faded. It had been buried, perhaps, pushed to the back of their minds as they tried to navigate the complexities of life. But now, in the wake of loss and personal crisis, that connection was surfacing again, stronger than ever. They didn't know if they would ever meet again, didn't know if the pact they had made so long ago still held any meaning. But in their hearts, they both knew that they were still tied to each other, that no matter how much time passed or how far apart they were, they would always be connected. The love they had shared was not bound by time or distance—it was a part of them, woven into the very fabric of their lives.

And so, as they each faced their own crises, Arjun and Meera found themselves thinking of the past, of the choices they had made, and of the love they had lost. They didn't know what the future held, but for the first time in a long time, they allowed themselves to hope that maybe, just maybe, the story wasn't over yet.

CHAPTER XV

THE ARCHITECTURE OF A NEW BEGINNING

Arjun strolled through the crowded aisles of the book fair, hands tucked into his pockets, his eyes skimming over the rows of book covers without really seeing them. The vibrant buzz of conversation, the smell of fresh paper and ink, the clamor of book lovers—it was all a strange contrast to the hollow silence he carried within. It had been a long time since he'd felt anything close to joy, but something about the energy of the book fair always pulled him in, like an echo of a life he once knew. Maybe it was nostalgia, maybe a faint hope of reconnecting with something he had lost. The weight of Ria's absence still clung to him, and the loss of their child had left an emptiness he couldn't describe. It was a wound so deep that even time couldn't seem to heal it. As the years had passed, he'd found solace in his work, in designing spaces that spoke to something timeless, something lasting, even as he felt like his own world was crumbling. His architecture had always been inspired by stories, by old-school love, by permanence. It was a way to hold on to things that he feared were slipping away.

Today, though, something felt different. As he moved through the fair, Arjun caught sight of a small girl standing alone near one of the book stalls. She couldn't have been more than seven or eight years old, her dark hair tied in a loose ponytail, her tiny hands clutching a book to her chest as if it were the most precious thing in the world. There was something about her—something in the way she stood, the quiet intensity in her eyes—that made Arjun stop.

The girl looked up at him, her gaze clear and unafraid, and for a moment, their eyes met. She held the book out to him, her small voice breaking through the noise around them. "Could you help me buy this, mister?"

Arjun blinked, caught off guard. He wasn't sure what it was about her request that struck him so deeply. Maybe it was the innocence in her voice, or the way her gaze held his with such quiet confidence. Without thinking, he knelt down to her level and gently took the book from her hands.

It was an old volume, well-worn and familiar. He turned it over, and his heart gave a painful jolt. It was the same book, *To Kill A Mockingbird* —the very same one that had brought him and Meera together all those years ago. He remembered the way they had met, how she had been flipping through the pages of this very book when they first spoke. It had been the beginning of everything, the start of something he had never fully let go of. Arjun looked at the girl again, this time more closely. She had the same wide, curious eyes that Meera had, the same quiet strength in the way she carried herself. A strange, almost surreal feeling washed over him, as if the universe was trying to tell him something, as if this moment held a significance he couldn't quite grasp.

"What's your name?" he asked softly.

The girl hesitated for a moment, then answered, "Maya."

"Maya," Arjun repeated, smiling faintly. "That's a beautiful name. Why do you want this book?"

Her gaze never wavered as she replied, "Because it makes me feel like I belong somewhere."

The simplicity of her answer hit him harder than he expected. It wasn't just the words, but the weight behind them, the unspoken loneliness that lingered there. He knew that feeling all too well.

"Where are your parents, Maya?" he asked gently, scanning the crowd for any sign of an adult looking for her.

She shrugged, her small shoulders rising and falling as if the question didn't really matter. "I don't know. I've been in lots of homes. But none of them are really mine."

The words settled heavily in the air between them, and something inside Arjun shifted. He saw himself in her, in the way she spoke, in the quiet resilience she carried. And suddenly, he realized that this wasn't just a random encounter. It was something more—a second chance.

Over the next few weeks, Arjun found himself returning to the book fair, looking for Maya in the sea of faces. Every time he saw her, they would talk, sometimes about books, sometimes about nothing at all. He learned that she loved stories, that she had a wild imagination, that she was endlessly curious about the world. But he also saw the sadness in her, the same sadness he carried in himself. It was an unspoken bond between them, one that neither of them fully understood but both seemed to need. The more time he spent with Maya, the more he felt something stirring in him—something he hadn't felt in a long time. It wasn't just a paternal instinct, though that was part of it. It was the realization that he had been given a chance to build something meaningful again, to create a new kind of love, a new kind of family. And as he grew closer to Maya, he began to think of her as more than just a child he had met by chance. He began to think of her as a daughter.

One day, after they had spent hours wandering through the book fair together, Arjun found himself kneeling down in front of her, his hands resting gently on her shoulders. "Maya," he said softly, "how would you feel about coming home with me?"

She looked at him, her dark eyes wide with surprise. "Home?" she repeated, as if the word were foreign to her.

Arjun nodded, his heart pounding in his chest. "Yes. I've been thinking... maybe we could make a home together. If you'd like that."

For a long moment, Maya said nothing. Then, slowly, a small smile spread across her face, and she nodded. "I'd like that," she whispered.

Arjun's heart swelled with emotion, and for the first time in years, he felt something like hope. As they walked away from the book fair that day, hand in hand, he knew that things would never be the same. He wasn't just building a house anymore. He was building a home.

In the months that followed, Arjun worked tirelessly to make his home a place where Maya could feel safe and loved. He decorated her room with soft colors, filled it with books and toys, and made sure there was always space for her imagination to roam. Slowly, he began to see his house not as a cold, empty space, but as a place where life could flourish again. Naming her wasn't a difficult choice. He knew from the moment he held her hand at that first book fair that there was only one name that felt right. Meera. Not just for the memory of the woman who had once filled his heart, but for the daughter he had never had, the family he had lost. It was a way to honour both Ria and Meera, to weave together the love he had known with the love he was creating.

"Meera," he whispered one night, as she slept soundly in her new bed, "you're home now."

The name felt right. It felt like healing. Like hope.

Time passed, and with it came moments of joy and pain, moments of growth and struggle. Arjun learned that being a father wasn't easy. There were days when he doubted himself, days when he wondered if he was doing the right thing, if he could ever truly fill the void in Maya's—Meera's—life. But then there were moments when she would smile at him, or tell him about a book she was reading, or curl up next to him on the couch with a quiet trust that made his heart swell.

In those moments, he knew that he had made the right choice.

As the years went by, Meera grew into a bright, curious young girl, full of life and laughter. She and Arjun would often go to the book fairs together, wandering through the stalls as they had that first day. It became their tradition, a way to connect, to remember the past while building a future together.

One day, as they were browsing through a particularly crowded stall, Meera picked up a book and handed it to Arjun. "This one," she said, her eyes shining with excitement. "It's the one you told me about, the one that brought you and... Maya...Meera together." Arjun took the book from her hands, his throat tightening. It was the same old volume, the one that had once connected him to Meera, and now, in a strange, serendipitous way, it had brought him and this Meera together too. He looked down at his daughter, her bright eyes watching him expectantly, and for a moment, he felt the weight of the past lift from his shoulders.

"It is," he whispered, his voice thick with emotion. "It is."

Meera smiled up at him, and in that moment, Arjun felt something shift inside him—a quiet peace, a sense of completeness he hadn't known in years. The pain of his past, the loss of Ria, the memories of Meera—they were still there, but they no longer held him captive. He had found something new, something real and alive in his daughter, something that gave him hope for the future. As they walked away from the stall, hand in hand, Arjun knew that his journey wasn't over. There were still parts of him that longed for the past, for the love he had lost. But now, he had something more—a reason to keep moving forward, a reason to keep building. And in Meera, both the memory and the present, he had found a new kind of love, one that wasn't bound by time or loss, but one that would carry him through whatever came next.

And for the first time in a long time, Arjun allowed himself to believe that maybe, just maybe, everything would be okay.

CHAPTER XVI

TAPESTRY OF LOVE AND MEMORY

Arjun often found himself staring at his daughter Meera with a sense of awe. Every time she curled up in her favorite chair, a book in hand, her hair falling over her eyes just like her mother's, he felt an odd mix of pride and melancholy. There was so much of her namesake in her, the Meera who had once been the love of his life, but this Meera, his daughter, was his reality. She was his constant, his little world, the one thing that tethered him to this life despite the heavy silence that settled within him on most days. Arjun had named her Meera for a reason. It wasn't something he spoke of, even when asked by his daughter. The subject was one he avoided, an unspoken boundary that both of them respected. But as Meera grew older, Arjun could see her curiosity growing too. She understood there was a story behind her name, behind her father's quiet grief and his long hours spent staring at old architecture sketches or flipping through books he never truly read. And though she didn't push, Meera became increasingly aware of how much her father's love for literature was tied to something—or rather, someone—she had never met.

At thirteen, Meera was already deep into her own world of books, much like Arjun had been at her age. She would disappear for hours, lost in the pages of classic novels, her mind alive with characters and stories that transported her to other worlds. Arjun had always wanted this for her—not just the joy of reading, but the ability to see the world through a literary lens, to understand life beyond the tangible, beyond the walls he built. She was growing into a thoughtful young woman, and though she didn't speak much about it, Arjun could see that she was beginning to grasp the connection between architecture and literature—the way both could tell a story, the way both could build and shape lives.

It wasn't lost on him how much his daughter resembled her namesake in spirit. She had the same quiet strength, the same curiosity about the world, the same love for language and art. But where the original Meera had been a bright star that he could never quite reach, his daughter Meera was a steady flame that illuminated his world, giving him purpose, keeping him moving forward. Even on his darkest days, when the weight of his loneliness felt unbearable, his daughter never failed to make him smile, to remind him that life still had something left to offer. Meera had developed a keen understanding of her father's work. She would often sit beside him as he pored over blueprints, asking questions about the buildings he designed, the stories behind them. "Dad, do you ever think of your designs as stories?" she asked one evening, her voice curious as she traced the lines of a sketch he was working on. "Like, the way a writer builds a world, you're building a space for people to live their lives in. Isn't that kind of the same thing?"

Arjun looked at her, startled by her insight. "I suppose it is," he said quietly. "Architecture is... it's about creating something that lasts. Something that tells a story long after we're gone."

Meera nodded, deep in thought. "Do you think your buildings reflect your life? Like, are they a part of you?"

He hesitated, unsure how to explain what he felt. "In a way, yes. Every building I design... it's influenced by something inside me. My experiences, my memories. The people I've loved."

It was a loaded statement, and Meera knew it. She didn't ask more, but she filed the conversation away in her mind, another piece of the puzzle that was her father's past.

In her own way, Meera was slowly uncovering the layers of her father's life. She had always sensed there was more to him than what he shared. His quietness, the way he carried himself with a kind of heaviness that never quite lifted, the way he looked at certain books on the shelves with an expression she couldn't decipher. And though he never spoke about her mother, Ria, or the Meera she was named after, his love for them was woven into the very fabric of their home.

The house they lived in was one of Arjun's earliest designs, and Meera often wondered if it was meant to be more than just a place to live. Every room seemed to hold a secret, a piece of a story that was left untold. The walls, with their intricate designs and subtle touches of old-world charm, felt like pages in a book that had been carefully written but never shared. She would run her fingers along the banisters, imagining the lives her father had built into the space, the love he had poured into every corner. As Meera grew older, she became more attuned to her father's emotional world. She saw the way he would retreat into his work when he was feeling particularly lonely, how he would lose himself in the blueprints as if they could somehow fill the void left by the people he had lost. But despite his quiet grief, Arjun was always there for her, always present in her life. He never let his sadness overshadow the love he had for his daughter, and in return, Meera made it her mission to be the light in his life.

"Dad, do you ever regret anything?" she asked one night, as they sat together in the living room, the soft glow of the fireplace casting shadows on the walls.

Arjun looked at her, surprised by the question. "Regret?" he repeated, his voice low.

Meera nodded. "Like, do you ever wish things had turned out differently?"

He was silent for a long time, his gaze distant. "Sometimes," he admitted finally. "But life... it doesn't always give us what we want. Sometimes, we have to make peace with what we have."

She thought about his words, the weight of them settling over her like a blanket. "But do you think... do you think we can still find happiness, even if things didn't go the way we wanted?"

Arjun smiled softly, his eyes filled with a kind of sadness that Meera was just beginning to understand. "I think happiness isn't about getting everything we want," he said. "It's about finding meaning in what we have."

Meera leaned her head against his shoulder, feeling the warmth of his presence, the steady beat of his heart. She didn't fully understand what he meant, but she knew that he was speaking from a place of deep experience, a place she had yet to reach. And in that moment, she realized just how much her father had given her—not just a home, but a love that transcended time and loss.

As the years went by, Meera continued to grow into her own person, her love for literature shaping her identity. She became a young woman with a sharp mind and a deep sense of empathy, someone who saw the world through both her father's eyes and her own. She began to understand that her father's life had been shaped by both joy and heartbreak, and though he never spoke of the people he had lost, their presence was always there, in the spaces he designed, in the stories he told through his work. But Meera never pushed. She respected the boundaries her father had set, knowing that some things were too painful to share. Instead, she honored his memory in her own way—by becoming the person he had always wanted her to be. She threw herself into her studies, becoming a master of words and stories, just as her father had hoped. And though she knew that her father's heart would always carry a quiet sadness, she made it her mission to fill their home with as much love and laughter as possible.

One day, as they sat together in the garden, Meera looked over at her father, a smile tugging at the corners of her lips. "Dad," she said softly, "do you ever think about how we met?"

Arjun looked at her, his expression tender. "Every day," he replied. "You were... you are the best thing that ever happened to me."

Meera's heart swelled with emotion, and for a moment, she saw her father not just as the man who had raised her, but as someone who had lived a life full of love and loss, someone who had given everything to make their home a place of peace and joy.

"I hope I'm making you proud," she said quietly, her voice filled with sincerity.

Arjun reached over, taking her hand in his. "You've always made me proud, Meera," he whispered. "Always."

And in that moment, Meera knew that no matter what had come before, no matter the pain and loss her father had endured, they had built something beautiful together—a bond that would last a lifetime, a love that would carry them through whatever the future held. In the quiet of their home, amidst the books and the stories that had shaped their lives, Arjun and Meera found peace. And though the past still lingered, it no longer held them captive. Instead, it was a part of the tapestry of their lives, woven into every moment of love and understanding they shared. She knew that her father's heart had enough room for both of them—for the memories of the past and the love they had built together. And in the end, that was all that mattered.

CHAPTER XVII

STORIES OF US

The wind carried with it the faint scent of rain, mingling with the crispness of autumn leaves as Meera sat by her window, her fingers lightly tracing the edge of a book she had just finished reading. The book, *The Will to Walk Forward,* was a revelation—a story of resilience and the will to move forward after profound loss. It spoke to her deeply, not just because of its poignant prose but because of the way it seemed to echo something unspoken in her own life. It was penned under a pseudonym, but the raw emotion and wisdom woven into the pages made it feel personal, almost like the writer had lived her own journey. Meera found herself clinging to the words, underlining passages that resonated, and reading certain sentences aloud as if hearing them would etch them more firmly into her heart. There was one in particular: *"We are more than the sum of what we have lost. We are the stories we choose to write with what remains."* It was the kind of wisdom her father often shared with her in quieter, more measured tones, but here, it was laid bare in black and white, giving her comfort in ways she didn't fully understand.

Her father, Arjun, was in the study, poring over designs for a new project, but Meera knew he wasn't entirely absorbed. She could tell when his mind wandered—his pencil paused mid-stroke, his eyes unfocused, staring beyond the sketches. She had learned to read these silences, understanding that they were part of the man her father was. She wanted to help him carry that weight, to ease the burdens he didn't speak of.

In her journal, she had written just last night:
> *"If love were a language, I'd learn its every word,*
> *If pain were a melody, I'd hum it unheard.*
> *For the heart of my father, I'd become a prayer,*
> *A bond unbroken, a life to share."*

Meera didn't know why the book had struck such a chord with her. Perhaps it was because the writer seemed to understand the delicate balance of carrying one's grief while still choosing to create something meaningful. Or perhaps it was the way the prose seemed to echo her father's unspoken thoughts—the quiet sadness he carried, the way he built worlds through his architecture yet seemed tethered to a past he rarely discussed. As she flipped through the pages once more, she made a mental note to tell her father about the book. But for now, she was content to savor its words alone, feeling as though they were a bridge between her own budding aspirations as a writer and her desire to honor her father's life.

Across the world, Meera, was in the middle of a packed lecture hall, her voice steady yet filled with an understated emotion that commanded attention. She had carved a life for herself in the world of literature, teaching and writing about the human condition and the intricate ways in which we navigate loss and love. Her work was widely respected, and her books—especially those written under her pseudonym—had gained a quiet but powerful following. It had been years since she last thought of Arjun in any tangible way, but his name still held a place in the corners of her mind. Occasionally, in the quiet moments between lectures or as she sipped her tea while revising a manuscript, memories of him would surface, soft and unbidden. She had long accepted that life had moved them in separate directions, but the imprint he had left on her was undeniable.

For Meera, writing under a pseudonym was both a way of protecting herself and of letting go. She poured her truths into her work, but she did so without the need for recognition. The stories she wrote were deeply personal, yet she distanced herself from them by hiding behind a name that wasn't hers. It gave her freedom, a way to honor her past without being consumed by it. Her most recent book, *The Will to Walk Forward*, was a culmination of years of reflection and growth. It wasn't about Arjun specifically, but his presence had undoubtedly influenced it. The themes of resilience, of creating beauty out of brokenness, were born from the life they had shared, however briefly. She didn't know who would read the book or what impact it would have, but she hoped it would offer solace to someone, somewhere.

And it did. The words she had written halfway across the globe found their way into the hands of a girl who bore her name, a girl whose father had built a life in her honor. Meera would never know the full extent of the connection, but it was there, a quiet thread tying them together.

For Arjun, seeing his daughter so engrossed in the book was a bittersweet moment. He recognized the title—it had been mentioned in one of his architecture journals, praised for its ability to weave stories of resilience with the metaphor of rebuilding. He hadn't read it himself, but seeing how it resonated with her darling made him curious. Yet, as he watched her underline passages and jot down notes in the margins, he couldn't bring himself to take the book from her hands. It was hers now, a part of her journey, just as certain books had once been a part of his. In the evenings, when the house was quiet except for the soft rustle of pages being turned, Arjun often thought about the parallel lives they led. Meera, her old love, wherever she was, must have moved on as he had, building a life out of what remained. He didn't dwell on the what-ifs anymore; it wasn't his way. But there were moments—brief, fleeting—when he wondered if she ever thought of him, if she remembered the way they had once shared a love of stories and spaces that felt like home.

Meera closed the book one night and walked to the study where her father was still sketching. "Dad," she said softly, holding the book to her chest, "have you ever read this?"

Arjun looked up, his eyes tired but kind. "Not yet," he admitted. "But I've heard it's good."

"It's more than good," she said, her voice filled with quiet conviction. "It's... it's like it was written for people like us. People who've lost something but still want to create something beautiful."

Her words struck him in a way she couldn't have

known. He set down his pencil and leaned back in his chair, studying her face—the earnestness in her eyes, the way she held the book as though it were a treasure. "You've always had a way with words," he said finally, his voice tinged with pride. "Maybe one day, you'll write something like that."

Meera smiled, her cheeks flushing slightly. "Maybe. But for now, I just want to keep learning. And... I want to make you proud."

"You already do," Arjun said, his voice steady but full of emotion. "Every single day."

She sat down beside him, placing the book on the table between them. "Do you think it's true? What the writer says about moving forward?"

"I think," he said carefully, "that moving forward doesn't mean forgetting. It means carrying the past with us in a way that helps us build something better."

Meera nodded, her fingers tracing the edges of the book. "I think so too."

In that moment, Arjun felt a quiet sense of gratitude. For his daughter, for the life they had built together, for the way she was growing into someone who could take the pieces of her world and turn them into something meaningful. And though he would never tell her, he saw so much of the other Meera in her—the way she loved words, the way she approached life with a mix of curiosity and quiet strength. As she continued to grow, she became more than just a daughter to Arjun. She became his confidante, his anchor, the one who kept him grounded when the weight of his memories threatened to pull him under. And though she didn't know the full story of her name or the depth of her father's past, she honored it in her own way—by living a life filled with love, resilience, and an unwavering devotion to the things that mattered most.

She often wrote letters to him, though she never gave them to him, using them as a way to process her thoughts. In one, she had written:

"Dear Dad,
You carry the weight of a thousand worlds,
Yet you never let it show.
I wish I could take some of that weight,
But all I can do is love you so.
You are my hero, my guide, my anchor,
And I am your humble shadow."

These letters became her private way of connecting with him, a tribute to the bond they shared.

On the other side of the world, Meera sat at her desk, finishing the final draft of her next book. As she typed the last sentence, she felt a quiet sense of fulfillment. She didn't know where the book would go or who it would reach, but she hoped it would find its way to someone who needed it. Perhaps, in some small way, it would bridge the gaps between lives, connecting hearts that were never meant to meet but were always meant to resonate. And so, across time and distance, the two Meeras—one a woman finding her way in the world, the other a girl discovering hers—continued to honor the stories that had shaped them, creating new ones in their wake. And at the heart of it all was Arjun, quietly proud, silently grateful, and deeply, irrevocably tied to them both.

THE VEIL OF QUIET TRUTHS

CHAPTER XVIII

A MEETING OF MINDS

The early morning mist hung like a veil over the bustling streets of Jaipur, where Meera found herself alongside her father on a trip that promised exploration, culture, and a touch of adventure. The city was alive with the sounds of honking rickshaws, the aroma of street food, and the chatter of eager travellers. This wasn't just another vacation—it was a chance to step out of their routine and immerse themselves in something new. Arjun, however, seemed less inclined toward sightseeing. He had spent the morning at their hotel, quietly working on a set of architectural sketches, leaving Meera free to explore. She had learned of a renowned book fair happening nearby, *The Jaipur Book Fair*, and her excitement was palpable. The event was said to draw some of the most celebrated authors, thinkers, and readers from across the globe. For a self-proclaimed bibliophile like Meera, it was nothing short of paradise.

"Are you sure you don't want to come, Dad?" she asked, standing by the hotel door with a tote bag slung over her shoulder.

Arjun smiled, his eyes filled with fondness. "I'll pass this time. You go ahead and enjoy. Bring back stories, okay?"

She nodded, kissed him on the cheek, and made her way out, her heart thrumming with anticipation. The Jaipur Literature Festival sprawled across the lawns of an old palace, its vibrant tents and colorful banners fluttering in the gentle breeze. The air buzzed with excitement as readers shuffled between stalls, authors gave talks on various stages, and the scent of freshly brewed coffee mingled with the perfume of old books.

Meera wandered through the maze of stalls, her eyes lighting up at the sight of her favorite authors' works and stacks of books that beckoned her to stop and browse. She attended a couple of talks, bought a few titles, and even managed to snag a signed copy of a poetry anthology. Yet, her heart yearned for more. She hoped against hope to meet the author behind *The Will to Walk Forward*, the book that had profoundly influenced her. Though the author used a pseudonym, rumors had been swirling about their possible attendance at this year's festival.

As fate would have it, her wish was about to come true.

On the other side of the fair, Meera was adjusting her scarf as she prepared for a small panel discussion. The festival had always been a place of inspiration for her—a convergence of minds and stories that fueled her own creativity. Though she kept her identity as the pseudonymous author carefully guarded, she couldn't resist interacting with readers who resonated with her work. She stepped out of the discussion tent, drawn to a quieter corner of the fair where a modest café offered respite from the crowd. Her gaze wandered over the tables, and she spotted a young woman poring over a book with an intensity that made her smile. She decided to sit at the adjacent table, her coffee in hand, intrigued by the quiet fervor of this reader.

Unbeknownst to her, the young woman was Meera (*Arjun's daughter Meera*).

Meera Jr. felt a presence beside her and looked up. "I hope I'm not disturbing you," the older woman said with a warm smile.

"Not at all," Meera replied, closing the book but keeping her finger between the pages. "It's just... this place is incredible. So many stories in one space."

"It is," the older woman agreed. "I come here every year. There's something magical about being surrounded by people who love words."

Their conversation began with the casual ease of two strangers who share a common passion. They discussed books, authors, and the power of storytelling. Meera found herself captivated by the older woman's depth of knowledge and her ability to articulate the very emotions Meera had often struggled to express. It was like talking to a kindred spirit, someone who understood not just her love for literature but the way it had shaped her life.

"What are you reading?" the woman asked.

Meera held up the book. *The Will to Walk Forward.*

The woman's eyes flickered with recognition, though she quickly masked it. "Ah, that one," she said, her voice tinged with affection. "What do you think of it?"

"It's..." Meera paused, searching for the right words. "It's like someone reached into my soul and put my feelings into sentences. The way it talks about loss and resilience—it's changed the way I see things. I've read it three times already."

The woman smiled. "It's always humbling to see how stories find their readers."

Meera tilted her head. "You seem to know a lot about it. Are you a fan of the author?"

"In a manner of speaking," the woman replied, a playful glint in her eyes. "Tell me, what draws you to this book in particular?"

Meera leaned forward, her enthusiasm bubbling over. "It's the honesty. The way the author doesn't sugarcoat grief but also doesn't let it consume the narrative. It's about moving forward, not as a way to forget but as a way to honor what you've lost. It's... it's exactly what I needed." For a moment, the woman's expression softened, and Meera thought she saw something unspoken in her eyes. But before she could dwell on it, their conversation veered into a discussion about other authors, genres, and the challenges of balancing creativity with life's practicalities.

Hours passed unnoticed as the two of them talked. They moved from the café to a quieter bench under a sprawling neem tree, their laughter mingling with the rustling leaves. It felt as though they had known each other forever, their shared love for literature bridging the gap between their ages and experiences. As the sun began to set, casting a golden glow over the fair, the woman checked her watch. "I should be heading back," she said reluctantly. "But before I go, there's something I should tell you."

Meera looked at her curiously.

"I'm the author of *The Will to Walk Forward*," the woman said, her voice calm but tinged with vulnerability. She gave Meera her pseudonym, careful not to reveal her real name.

Meera's jaw dropped. "You're... you wrote this?" she asked, holding up the book with reverence.

The woman nodded. "I did."

For a moment, Meera was too stunned to speak. Then, a wide smile broke across her face. "I can't believe this. You have no idea how much your work means to me. It's changed my life."

"Thank you," the woman said, her voice thick with emotion. "That means more than you know."

As they stood to part ways, Meera extended her hand. "My name is Meera," she said.

The older woman froze for a split second, the name hitting her like a jolt. She recovered quickly, smiling as she shook Meera's hand. "It's a beautiful name," she said, her voice steady but her mind reeling.

That night, back at the hotel, Meera burst into her father's study, her face alight with excitement. "Dad, you won't believe who I met today!"

Arjun looked up, surprised by her enthusiasm. "Who?"

"The author of *The Will to Walk Forward*!" she said, holding up the book. "She's amazing, Dad. We talked for hours about books and life and everything in between. It felt like... I don't know, like meeting a kindred spirit."

Arjun smiled, his heart swelling with pride and affection. "I'm glad you had such a good day," he said, though he couldn't shake the feeling that there was more to the story.

For the other Meera, the encounter stayed with her long after she returned to her hotel room. The young woman's name and the spark in her eyes haunted her, filling her with a mix of emotions she couldn't quite untangle. She didn't know who she was or what her connection to the name might be, but she felt an inexplicable bond with the girl—a sense that their meeting was more than coincidence. In the days that followed, both Meeras' found themselves thinking back to that fateful day at the book fair. For Meera Jr., it was the start of a mentorship that would shape her writing and her worldview. For Meera Sr., it was a reminder of the power of connection and the ways in which their lives continued to intersect, even unknowingly.

And for Arjun, it was another thread in the tapestry

of his life—a quiet, unspoken link between the two Meeras' who had shaped his world in ways he could never fully articulate.

CHAPTER XIX

BETWEEN PAGES AND PROMISES

The brisk morning air carried the scent of freshly brewed coffee as Meera Jr. sat in a quiet corner of the café nestled within the bookfair grounds. The festival was in full swing, its vibrant chaos spilling into every tent and stall, but she craved a moment of stillness to sip her coffee and gather her thoughts. A notebook lay open before her, its pages filled with scribbled ideas and half-written paragraphs. She had been working on this piece for months now, pouring her heart into every word. It wasn't just another essay or story—it was a tribute to her father, a man who had carried the weight of loss with a quiet dignity and had built a life of warmth and resilience. She wanted the article to capture his essence, his unyielding spirit, and the love that defined their bond. Yet, writing it felt like baring her soul, and she wasn't ready to show it to anyone. Not yet.

Her thoughts were interrupted by the arrival of a familiar voice.

"Lost in your world again, I see," Meera Sr. said, a playful smile dancing on her lips as she approached the table.

Meera Jr. looked up, her face lighting up. "I guess you caught me," she said, closing her notebook instinctively, her cheeks flushing.

It had been a few months since their first meeting at the Jaipur festival, and though their interactions were rare and limited to these serendipitous moments, they had formed a connection that felt strangely natural. Meera Jr. looked up to the older woman as a mentor, someone who seemed to understand her aspirations and struggles without needing much explanation.

The older woman sat down across from her, placing a steaming cup of tea on the table. "Still working on that secret project of yours?" she teased gently.

Meera hesitated, torn between her instinct to keep the article private and her growing trust in the woman she had come to admire. "Sort of," she admitted. "It's about someone close to me. Someone who's been... everything to me."

Meera Sr. raised an eyebrow, intrigued but cautious not to pry. "Sounds like a beautiful subject. I hope I get to read it someday."

Their conversations often took this tone—deep enough to hint at the heart of their thoughts but careful not to cross the boundaries of their guarded lives. Over the course of their interactions, they had developed an unspoken understanding. Meera Sr. admired the younger woman's passion for writing and her earnest desire to tell stories that mattered, while Meera Jr. found herself drawn to the older woman's wisdom and her ability to weave words into something transformative.

What neither of them realized was how much they mirrored each other.

For Meera Sr., these moments felt like a bittersweet echo of the life she had imagined years ago. She often caught herself marveling at how similar Meera Jr. was to the daughter she had once dreamed of having. The younger woman's sharp wit, her gentle compassion, and even the way she held her pen—it all stirred something deep within her. But she never allowed herself to dwell on those thoughts for too long. To reveal her past, her identity, would be to open a door she had long since locked. It was easier, safer, to exist in this liminal space, where they were simply two lovers of literature sharing fleeting conversations.

As the festival days passed, Meera Jr. found herself drawn to the older woman's tent. They would sit for hours, discussing everything from classic novels to modern poetry, their conversations flowing effortlessly. But there was one topic Meera Jr. couldn't resist bringing up—her father. "My dad is my hero," she confessed one afternoon, her eyes shining with pride. "He's the reason I'm here today, pursuing my passion. He's been through so much, but he's never let it make him bitter. He's the strongest person I know."

Meera Sr. listened intently, her chest tightening at the words. Though the younger woman didn't say his name, her descriptions painted a vivid picture—one that was hauntingly familiar.

"He's an architect," Meera Jr. continued. "But I think he's an artist at heart. The way he sees the world, the way he builds... it's like he's trying to create something beautiful out of the broken pieces of life."

The older woman's breath hitched, but she masked it with a sip of tea. "He sounds extraordinary," she said softly.

"He is," Meera Jr. said with a smile. "I'm writing about him, actually. It's my first real piece, and it means everything to me. I want the world to see him the way I do."

The article had become her labor of love, a secret she guarded fiercely. She hadn't even told her father about it. But sharing bits and pieces with Meera Sr. felt like the right thing to do, even if she didn't know why.

On the final day of the festival, they met again, this time in a quieter corner of the gardens. Meera Jr. carried a draft of her article, though she wasn't sure if she was ready to share it. They talked as they always did, but there was an undercurrent of something deeper in their words.

"What drives you to write?" Meera Sr. asked suddenly, her gaze fixed on the younger woman.

Meera Jr. thought for a moment before replying. "I think it's love," she said finally. "Love for the people who've shaped me, for the stories that deserve to be told. Writing feels like the only way to make sense of it all."

The older woman nodded, her eyes glistening with unshed tears. "That's a beautiful answer," she said. "And it's exactly why you'll go far. Writing with love is the only way to reach people's hearts."

Encouraged by her words, Meera Jr. pulled out the folded pages of her draft and hesitated before handing them over. "Would you... would you read it?" she asked.

Meera Sr. took the pages, her hands trembling slightly. "I'd be honored," she said.

Later that evening, as she sat in her hotel room, Meera Sr. unfolded the pages and began to read. The words wove themselves into her mind, filled with admiration and gratitude, painting a vivid picture of a man who had faced profound loss and yet managed to build a life full of love and purpose for his daughter. She read about his sacrifices, his quiet strength, and the way he taught his child to find beauty in a world that often felt fractured. Each sentence resonated with a depth that tugged at her heart.

Her gaze lingered on a particular passage:

"He once told me that life is like architecture—you take what's given to you, and you build something meaningful. He's done that for me, and I hope to do the same for him."

The words sent a jolt through her, their familiarity tightening her chest. Her breath caught as a fleeting thought took hold—a thought she tried to dismiss as quickly as it came. *Could it be Arjun?*

For a moment, the possibility consumed her. The description, the wisdom in those words—they were too similar, too aligned with the man she had once known so intimately. It felt as though the universe was playing a cruel trick, dangling fragments of her past before her only to remind her of all she had lost. But then she shook her head and forced herself to breathe. *No,* she thought. *It's not possible.* Life didn't work that way. Arjun belonged to a chapter long closed, a story written in a different time. The chances that this young woman's father was the same man who had been at the heart of her past were too slim, too absurd to entertain. Still, as she hurried through the rest of the draft, trying to shake the feeling, memories of her promise to Arjun surfaced unbidden. The pact they had made in their youth—the one that felt so distant, like a whisper in the wind—now pressed heavily on her mind.

Maybe this was the universe's way of reminding me of that day, she thought. A gentle nudge to honor her past, not by unraveling it, but by finding the courage to face it.

The thought settled deep within her. If nothing else, this encounter had stirred something she hadn't felt in years. A quiet resolve began to take root—a desire to find Arjun and bring clarity to the fragments of memory still tethered to her heart. The next morning, they met one last time before parting ways. Meera Jr. was eager to hear her thoughts on the article, but the older woman only smiled and handed it back.

"It's beautiful," she said simply. "Your father will be so proud."

Meera Jr. beamed at the praise, her heart swelling with joy. "Thank you," she said. "It means a lot coming from you."

As they hugged goodbye, neither of them spoke of the truth that lingered between them. Meera Jr. didn't know the depth of their connection, and Meera Sr. couldn't bring herself to reveal it.

But as they walked away from each other, each carrying the weight of their unspoken truths, they both felt a sense of peace.

For Meera Sr., it was enough to know that life wanted her to honor her past and be the person she, now that she has achieved her dream as a writer, she should follow her heart and wait. And for Meera Jr., it was enough to have found a guide who understood her heart and her love for words.

And somewhere in the spaces between their lives,

Arjun's memory lived on, quietly binding them together in ways they could never fully comprehend.

THE FRAMEWORKS OF MEMORY

The article, titled *A Father's Architecture of Love*, was released under the pseudonym "Illusion" and instantly struck a chord with readers worldwide. Meera Jr.'s words danced across the pages, painting an evocative portrait of a man whose life had been etched into the lines and corners of his architectural masterpieces. The article was not just a tribute to Arjun's work but a profound exploration of his character as seen through his daughter's eyes. It spoke of resilience, compassion, and an enduring love that had built not just homes and spaces but also a safe haven for a young girl finding her way in the world. The piece gained traction quickly. Academics, critics, and casual readers alike marveled at its depth. It was raw, tender, and poetic—each word weighed with emotion yet unburdened by sentimentality. Meera Jr. had managed to intertwine her father's professional brilliance with his personal sacrifices, presenting a man whose architecture was as much about constructing physical spaces as it was about holding together the fragile pieces of their life.

"Buildings are like people," one section read. "They carry histories in their cracks, dreams in their foundations, and love in the spaces they create. My father is no different. He built a life for us out of ruins, one beam of strength at a time, and though he says he is proud of me, I will forever be in awe of him." The article was both a gift and a revelation, even to those who thought they knew Arjun's work. His designs, critiqued and celebrated for years, now carried new meaning when viewed through the lens of his daughter's words.

Arjun discovered the article unexpectedly. Meera Jr. had kept it a surprise, waiting for the perfect moment to share it with him, but the world's acclaim reached him before she could. Sitting at his desk, reviewing blueprints for a new project, he had opened his email to find a link sent by a colleague who had described the article as "a piece that breathes life into architecture."

He clicked on it, curious but unsuspecting, and as the words unfolded before him, he felt his breath hitch. By the third paragraph, he had set his glasses aside, the blueprints forgotten. Tears welled in his eyes as he read her descriptions of their life together, her quiet admiration for the sacrifices he thought went unnoticed. She spoke of his hands, calloused from years of work, as symbols of resilience. She spoke of the way he taught her to look at the world—not just as it was, but as it could be.

"She sees me," he whispered, voice breaking. "She really sees me."

His heart swelled with pride, but beneath it lay a deep, aching tenderness. In her words, he glimpsed the life they had built together, a life that had not always been easy but was undeniably full of love. Finishing the article, Arjun leaned back in his chair, overwhelmed. Memories flooded his mind—long nights spent sketching designs by lamplight, the sound of Meera's laughter filling their small apartment, the quiet evenings they spent reading side by side. He thought of Ria, her brief but impactful presence in their lives, and the ways she had shaped Meera into the compassionate young woman she had become. He thought of the other Meera, the one whose name he had given to his daughter, and the promise he had made years ago.

"Find me when you've built your world, and I'll find you when I've built mine."

He chuckled ruefully, wiping his eyes. Life had built many things, but it had not brought them back together. And yet, as he looked at his daughter's words, he couldn't help but feel that Meera Sr.'s influence was still alive somehow, carried like an unseen thread through their lives.

When Meera Jr. walked into the room later that evening, he was still holding the printout of the article. She looked at him, then at the paper, her face breaking into a shy smile.

"You found it," she said softly.

"I did," he replied, pulling her into a hug. "And I don't have enough words to tell you how proud I am of you."

They sat together for hours that night, the article sparking conversations about their shared journey, their memories, and their dreams for the future. For Arjun, it was a reminder of all he had gained, even amidst the losses that had once felt insurmountable.

Across the world, in a quiet study surrounded by books, Meera came across the article by chance. A literary acquaintance had forwarded it to her, praising the emotional depth of the piece and urging her to read it. As she began to read, her interest turned into awe. The words felt familiar, not just in their tone but in their essence. The writer, clearly young and passionate, carried a voice that reminded her of her own youthful zeal, someone who could relate to her own namesake.

But it wasn't just the writing style that struck her. It was the subject of the article. The man it described—a resilient architect, a father who had endured unimaginable loss—felt almost too real. She paused midway through, her hands trembling slightly. *It can't be,* she told herself. *It's just a coincidence.*

Yet, the vivid details and the metaphors used to describe his work tugged at memories she had long buried. The phrase about life being like architecture sent a shiver down her spine. It was something she had heard before, long ago, from someone she had never truly forgotten. She closed the article and leaned back in her chair, her mind racing. Could this father really be *him?* The thought felt absurd. Life didn't work that way. People moved on, lives diverged, and the threads of old connections frayed and broke.

But as much as she tried to dismiss it, the idea lingered, refusing to fade. She thought of Meera Jr.— her passion for literature, her warmth, her uncanny ability to connect with people through words, all evident in the article.

Her thoughts turned to the promise she had made to Arjun, the one she had carried like a quiet whisper in her heart all these years.

"Find me when you've built your world, and I'll find you when I've built mine."

Had the time come to fulfill it?

She didn't have an answer, but she knew one thing: meeting Meera Jr. had stirred something in her—a desire not just to honor the past but to face it.

For Meera Jr., the article was more than just her first published work; it was a piece of her soul laid bare. She didn't know how deeply it would resonate with the two people whose lives had shaped her the most. To her father, it was a validation of his journey, a testament to the life he had built against all odds. To Meera Sr., it was a bittersweet reminder of the life she had left behind and the connections she had lost. Between the two of them, Meera Jr. stood as a bridge—a living embodiment of love, resilience, and the unspoken bond that connected their worlds. And though neither Arjun nor Meera Sr. could have foreseen the role she would play in their lives, both found themselves drawn to her light, grateful for the way she carried their stories forward. In her, they saw not just a reflection of themselves but the hope of a future that honored the past while embracing the possibilities of what lay ahead. And in her words, they found the courage to take one step closer to the paths they had once left behind.

CHAPTER XXI

The Unfinished Room

The quiet hum of the ceiling fan filled the room, a soft backdrop to Arjun's thoughts as he sat by the window, the faint glow of twilight brushing against his facc. His hands rested lightly on the worn wooden arms of his chair, but his mind was anything but still. It drifted between fragments of his past and the peculiar anticipation of what lay ahead—a meeting he wasn't even sure would happen. Life had taught him patience in ways he hadn't imagined. There was a time when he might have rushed headlong into things, seeking closure or answers. But now, with years of reflection behind him, he knew that some things couldn't be hurried. Especially not this.

The promise he and Meera had made to each other all those years ago was a tender memory he carried with care. It wasn't an obligation or a weight; it was a quiet, steady truth that had been a compass in his life. The idea of meeting her now was as exhilarating as it was unnerving. He had spent years building a life he could be proud of, one that honored the very spirit of that promise. Architecture had become his canvas, but it was more than a career—it was his way of holding together the fragmented pieces of his heart and past.

He leaned forward slightly, his gaze falling on the small stack of books on the desk across the room. Among them was a journal, its leather binding cracked and softened with age. He reached for it instinctively, his fingers brushing over the cover before opening it to a blank page. Writing had become a quiet companion in his solitude, a place where he could sift through his thoughts without fear of judgment. He hesitated for a moment before penning the first words:

"Life feels like architecture. The structure is built on the foundation of choices, memories, and the spaces we leave for others. Meeting her feels like walking into an unfinished room,

unsure of what it might hold but knowing it's a part of the home I've built within myself."

He paused, rereading the words. It was true—his feelings for Meera were not driven by longing in the romantic sense. What he felt was gratitude, a deep and abiding respect for the way she had shaped him. She had given him the courage to move forward when everything else had felt insurmountable. And yet, he couldn't deny the doubts that crept in. What if she didn't come? What if she had moved on so completely that their promise was little more than a distant, forgotten memory to her? What if their lives were now too different to bridge the gap between them?

He closed the journal softly, his fingers lingering on the edge of the page. Doubts were a natural part of this process, he told himself. But they couldn't outweigh the quiet, persistent hope that had sustained him all these years. Arjun rose from his chair, pacing the room slowly. The familiar surroundings—the bookshelf, the intricate model of a building he had once designed, the framed photograph of him and Meera Jr. from years ago—offered a kind of comfort. But his mind wandered beyond the confines of the room, back to the days when he and Meera Sr. had shared dreams and laughter, building a connection that felt as natural as breathing.

He could still hear her voice sometimes, not in a haunting way but as a soft echo that reminded him of the way she had encouraged him to see the world differently. She had been more than a muse; she had been a mirror reflecting his best and truest self. The years hadn't erased the sharp edges of their parting, but they had softened them. He no longer dwelled on what might have been, finding instead a quiet acceptance of what was. Meera Sr. had been an integral part of his story, but she wasn't its ending.

Looking out the window now, he allowed himself a small smile. He was content with his life—the work he did, the bond he shared with his daughter, the sense of purpose he carried in his heart. And yet, the idea of seeing Meera again brought a sense of wonder he hadn't felt in a long time. That evening, as he sat down to dinner with Meera Jr., she noticed the quiet look in his eyes.

"Everything okay, Papa?" she asked, her voice filled with concern.

He nodded, offering her a reassuring smile. "Just thinking," he said.

"About what?"

"About how far we've come," he replied. "And how much farther we still have to go."

She smiled at that, her eyes lighting up with the warmth that always reminded him of Ria. His daughter was his greatest achievement, the living embodiment of the love and resilience he had poured into their lives.

"You always say such profound things," she teased, breaking the serious mood. "It's like living with a philosopher."

"Architects and philosophers aren't so different," he said with a wink.

Later that night, as she retired to her room, Arjun found himself standing in front of the bookshelf. His fingers traced the spines of books he hadn't touched in years, finally landing on one that Meera Sr. had once gifted him. Pulling it out, he opened it to the first page, where her handwriting greeted him like an old friend.

"To Arjun, for the architect of dreams. May your work always inspire."

He sat down with the book, flipping through its pages as memories washed over him. It wasn't sadness he felt, but a deep, bittersweet appreciation for everything they had shared.

The following days were filled with a quiet kind of preparation. He didn't know how the meeting would happen, but he wanted to be ready—for himself, for her, and for the promise they had made. He began sorting through old sketches and designs, pulling out the ones that had been inspired by his time with her. Some of them were unfinished, just as their story had been. Others had evolved into full-fledged projects, shaped by the years that followed.

As he worked, he found himself thinking about the kind of life they might have had if things had been different. It wasn't regret that filled him but a kind of wistful curiosity. The "what-ifs" were there, but they didn't overshadow the gratitude he felt for the life he had built—a life that honored the spirit of their promise. He thought about the impact she had on him, not just as a partner but as a person. She had taught him to see the world through a lens of possibility, to embrace creativity and vulnerability in equal measure. And now, as he prepared to meet her again, he felt a renewed sense of purpose.

The days were drawing closer, Arjun found himself sitting at his desk, pen in hand. He began writing a letter—not for her, but for himself.

"Dear Meera,

I don't know if you'll come. And I don't know if I'll have the courage to say everything I want to if you do. But I want you to know that you changed my life. You gave me the strength to move forward, to build something meaningful, and to find joy even in the midst of loss.

You once said that life is like architecture. You were right. And the life I've built is better for having known you."
He stopped writing, folding the paper and tucking it into his journal. It wasn't something he planned to give her, but it felt good to put his feelings into words. As he sat back, a sense of calm washed over him. Whatever happened tomorrow, he knew he was ready. His journey with Meera had already been a gift, and this meeting—if it happened—would be a chance to honor that. For now, all he could do was wait, trusting in the promise they had made and the life they had each built in its wake.

CHAPTER XXII

The Letter and the Light

Meera sat in her study, the golden hues of the setting sun pouring through the half-drawn curtains. The light cast long shadows on the walls, accentuating the shelves lined with books, each one holding a piece of her life's journey. She gently placed her cup of tea on the side table, her hands lingering on the rim of the porcelain for a moment as her thoughts wandered back in time.

Arjun.

The name had lived in the quiet corners of her heart, not as a wound but as a constant—a soft hum that resonated with the rhythm of her life. He had been the cornerstone of her dreams, a figure whose presence had once given her the strength to push forward when everything seemed to stand still. She had built her life on the foundation of what they had shared, and though time had distanced them, his influence remained etched in her every achievement. She leaned back in her chair, closing her eyes as memories unfolded like pages of an old book. She remembered the late-night conversations that had stretched until dawn, the way they had shared ideas and dreams as if the world outside didn't exist. Arjun had been her confidant, her muse, and her anchor. Even in his absence, she had clung to the belief that what they had shared was real, pure, and enduring.

But now, after all these years, the prospect of seeing him again stirred something unfamiliar in her.

It wasn't fear or anxiety—it was something deeper, more nuanced. Meera wasn't sure if it was excitement, hesitation, or a bittersweet combination of both. She had always imagined Arjun as a guiding force in her life, someone whose memory had propelled her forward. Meeting him in person again felt like stepping into a dream she had replayed countless times in her mind, except now it was real, tangible, and entirely unpredictable. Her life had been full—filled with accomplishments, recognition, and the satisfaction of nurturing countless students who had gone on to shape the literary world. But amidst all that, there had always been an undercurrent of "what if." Not regret, but a quiet curiosity about what life might have looked like if she and Arjun had stayed in each other's lives.

Meera rose from her chair and walked over to her desk, where a worn notebook lay open. It was her personal journal, a sanctuary where she had poured her thoughts over the years. Flipping through its pages, she found a passage she had written long ago:

"Love isn't always about possession or permanence. Sometimes, it's the force that pushes you to become who you're meant to be. Arjun was that force for me—a constant reminder of what I could achieve, of the beauty in the world even when it felt out of reach."

She smiled faintly as she read the words, feeling their truth resonate even now. She had loved Arjun, not in the conventional sense that demanded reciprocation or permanence, but in a way that had allowed her to grow. He had been the wind beneath her wings, even when he wasn't physically there. Meera thought back to the promise they had made—to meet again one day, when the time was right after forty years. At the time, it had seemed like a distant, almost whimsical idea. But now, as the day approached, she couldn't help but wonder what it would be like to see him again. Would he recognize the person she had become? Would she see traces of the Arjun she remembered in the man he was now?

She wasn't naïve; she knew that time changed people. The years they had spent apart had undoubtedly shaped them in ways neither of them could predict. And yet, there was a part of her that hoped—hoped that the essence of who they were to each other had remained unchanged. But with that hope came caution. Meera had built a life that she was proud of, a life that stood as a testament to her resilience and determination. She didn't want this meeting to disrupt the balance she had worked so hard to achieve. She loved Arjun for who he had been to her—a guide, an inspiration, and a quiet source of strength. She wasn't sure if she was ready for him to become anything more than that.

The days leading up to their potential meeting were

filled with a strange mix of anticipation and introspection. Meera found herself revisiting old memories, not to dwell on the past but to understand the person she had been and the person she had become. She thought about the times she had struggled to find her footing in the literary world, the countless nights spent drafting and redrafting manuscripts that never seemed good enough. It was Arjun's encouragement that had kept her going, even from afar. She remembered the way he had believed in her, often more than she had believed in herself. And yet, she had never allowed herself to become dependent on his memory. Arjun was a part of her story, but he wasn't its entirety. She had learned to stand on her own, to find strength in her voice and purpose in her work. Meeting him now felt like closing a circle, not reopening old wounds.

One evening, as she sat in her study, Meera picked up a pen and began writing a letter. She didn't know if she would ever give it to Arjun, but the act of writing felt cathartic.

"Dear Arjun,

I don't know what the future holds or what this meeting will bring, but I want you to know that you've been a part of my life in ways you can't imagine. You were the spark that ignited my passion for literature, the steady hand that guided me even when you weren't there.

I've often wondered what our lives might have looked like if things had been different. But over the years, I've come to realize that the beauty of what we shared lies in its impermanence. You were a chapter in my story, but you helped me write the rest of the book.

If we meet again, I hope it's as two people who have lived full lives, who have grown and changed but still recognize the bond that brought them together. Whatever happens, know that I am grateful—for you, for us, and for everything that came after."

She folded the letter carefully and tucked it into her journal, feeling a sense of peace wash over her. The meeting wasn't about rekindling old flames or rewriting the past; it was about honoring the journey they had both taken and the ways they had shaped each other's lives.

As the day approached, Meera found herself oscillating between excitement and trepidation. She knew that Arjun had played a pivotal role in her life, but she also knew that she had changed. The girl who had once leaned on him for support had grown into a woman who stood tall on her own. She wasn't sure what she would say when they met or how she would feel seeing him again. But she knew one thing for certain: she was ready. Ready to face the past, to embrace the present, and to step into whatever the future held.

In the quiet moments before sleep, Meera allowed herself to imagine the meeting. She pictured Arjun's face, older but still familiar, his eyes holding the same warmth and kindness she remembered. She imagined the conversations they would have, the stories they would share, and the quiet understanding that would pass between them. But more than anything, she felt a sense of gratitude—for the journey that had brought her here, for the person she had become, and for the promise that had remained a constant in her life.

CHAPTER XXIII

THE PROMISE UNFOLDS

The years had slipped by like pages turning in a book, each one filled with its own trials and triumphs, joys and sorrows, yet always underpinned by the quiet echo of a promise made long ago. Time had not been kind in its relentlessness, yet it had allowed both Meera and Arjun to grow, to create, to live.

Meera Sr., now a celebrated figure in the literary world, had carved a life out of words. Her stories, rich with emotion and brimming with authenticity, touched countless lives. She became a voice for the voiceless, a beacon for those seeking meaning in the chaos of existence. Awards adorned her walls, accolades she never sought but quietly appreciated. To the world, she was a luminary, a mentor, a guide. To herself, she remained the woman who had once loved deeply and lost, carrying the memory of that love like a hidden gem, its luster undiminished by time. In her solitude, Meera found solace in her work. She nurtured young writers, poured her heart into her books, and built a legacy of resilience and creativity. Yet, late at night, when the world was quiet, her thoughts would drift back to him—Arjun. His presence lingered in her mind like an unfinished poem, its lines etched in the language of what-ifs and might-have-been. She never allowed herself to dwell too long on those memories, but they were there, shaping her, inspiring her. She had loved him not with the fervor of possession but with the quiet strength of gratitude. He had been her foundation, her guiding star, and though their paths diverged, the light he cast never dimmed.

Arjun, too, had built a life of meaning. His journey as an architect was not without challenges, but he faced them with unwavering determination. His creations stood tall, structures that blended form and function, inspired by the same principles that had guided his life. He often thought of architecture as a metaphor, a way to shape something meaningful out of whatever materials life offered. It was a philosophy born from his conversations with Meera, one that had stayed with him as he worked tirelessly to provide for his daughter. Meera Jr. had been the center of his universe, the reason he rose each day with purpose. He had played the dual roles of father and mother, pouring all his love and energy into raising her. There were sacrifices, yes—moments of loneliness, nights spent working late, dreams deferred—but there was also an unparalleled joy in watching her grow into a confident, compassionate young woman. She reminded him of Meera Sr. in ways he couldn't articulate, her spirit a reflection of the woman who had once been his muse. Still, the past was never far from his mind. Arjun often found himself wondering what might have been if life had unfolded differently. Yet, he never allowed regret to consume him. Instead, he chose gratitude—for the love he had known, for the lessons it had taught him, and for the life it had led him to create.

The passage of time brought with it moments of reflection. Meera Sr., in her quiet moments, would sift through old letters, her fingers tracing the faded ink of words exchanged long ago. She never read them aloud; they were too sacred, too personal. They were fragments of a life she had left behind yet carried with her. In those letters, she found not only the voice of a younger Arjun but also her own—a woman filled with hope, ambition, and a belief in the power of love. That woman still lived within her, tempered by the wisdom and scars of experience. For Arjun, his memories surfaced in the spaces between his daily routines. The quiet of his study, the rustle of paper as he sketched, the warmth of his daughter's laughter—all these moments carried echoes of Meera. He never spoke of her to Meera Jr.; it wasn't a secret but a sanctuary, a part of his life that was his alone. Yet, his daughter's presence often reminded him of the promise he had made all those years ago, a promise that had shaped him even as it remained unfulfilled.

Their lives, though separate, seemed to dance around each other in a quiet, unspoken rhythm. Meera Sr. would read about architectural marvels in the newspapers, her mind involuntarily tracing back to Arjun. Was he behind these creations? She never sought to find out. The mystery was comforting, a reminder that some connections didn't need confirmation to be real. Meanwhile, Arjun occasionally came across her name in literary circles, her words resonating with him even when he didn't know they were hers. He admired her from afar, not as a lost love but as a kindred spirit whose influence he still felt. Over the years, both had turned to writing as a way to process their emotions. Meera Sr.'s journals were filled with reflections on love, loss, and resilience, while Arjun's sketches often carried annotations that were more poetic than technical. In these private spaces, they allowed themselves to be vulnerable, to confront the emotions they otherwise kept at bay.

Letters, too, played a role in bridging the years. Meera Sr. wrote to no one in particular, her words spilling onto the page as if she were speaking to an old friend. She never sent them but kept them in a drawer, a collection of thoughts and feelings too precious to share. Arjun, on the other hand, wrote sporadic letters addressed to Meera Sr., though he never intended for her to see them. They were his way of honoring the promise he had made, a quiet acknowledgment of the role she continued to play in his life. As the decades unfolded, their lives bore the marks of growth and change. Meera Sr. became a mentor, her influence shaping a new generation of writers. She found joy in their successes, a reminder that her work was not in vain. Yet, there was an undercurrent of solitude in her life, a space that no accolades or accomplishments could fill.

Arjun found fulfillment in his daughter's achievements, her successes a testament to the love and effort he had poured into her upbringing. She became his legacy, the embodiment of all he had hoped to achieve. Yet, in quiet moments, he would trace the lines of a sketch or reread an old letter, and the memories of Meera would rise to the surface, unbidden but welcome. Their journeys, though separate, were bound by the invisible threads of shared ideals and mutual inspiration. They had loved each other in a way that transcended time and space, their connection a testament to the enduring power of genuine affection and respect. As the years turned into decades, the promise they had made to meet again became less about fulfilling an obligation and more about honoring the bond they shared.

And so, as the 40th year approached, both Meera Sr. and Arjun found themselves looking back on their lives with a sense of gratitude and anticipation. The promise lingered in their minds, not as a burden but as a beacon, guiding them toward a moment they both knew would be significant. They didn't know what the future held or if the meeting would bring closure or new beginnings. But they both felt the pull of destiny, a quiet certainty that their paths would cross once more. In the tapestry of their lives, time had been both a thief and a gift. It had taken away the immediacy of their connection but had given them the space to grow, to build, to become. As they stood on the cusp of the 40th year, they carried with them not only the weight of the past but also the hope of what might come next.

The years had passed, but the promise remained. And in their hearts, they knew that some stories were never truly over.

THREADS OF ETERNITY

CHAPTER XXIV

THE NIGHT BEFORE

The evening before the meeting was drenched in the kind of silence that made every thought louder, every memory more vivid. Meera Sr. sat at her desk, the soft light of the lamp casting a golden hue on the collection of letters and mementos spread before her. Her fingers trembled slightly as they traced the edges of an old envelope, its paper worn and delicate. She hadn't meant to revisit these relics of her past, but they had found her tonight, demanding her attention. The letters were a tapestry of a different time, fragments of conversations exchanged between two people who had once dreamed together. In the quiet of her study, she unfolded one of them and read Arjun's handwriting, its firm strokes still carrying the echoes of his voice. The words transported her to moments when the future felt full of promise, unburdened by the weight of what had yet to be lost.

She folded the letter carefully and placed it back in the box, her heart heavy yet hopeful. **Will he come?** The thought had haunted her all day. She had no guarantees, only the fragile thread of a promise made forty years ago. Forty years—it felt like both a lifetime and a heartbeat. Could two people who had lived so much apart still recognize each other? Would he see in her the woman he had once loved, or would she be a stranger now, shaped by time and distance?

Her heart quickened as she thought of the next day. Meera was a woman known for her composure, her ability to command rooms and inspire others, yet tonight, she felt like a nervous young girl. She had picked out her outfit carefully, a sari in soft shades of ivory and gold, elegant yet understated. It wasn't vanity driving her choices but the desire to feel like herself, the version of herself she had been when they last met. She glanced at the clock—it was nearing midnight. Outside her window, the city was alive with its usual rhythms, but inside her home, the world had narrowed to just this moment, this anticipation. She caught her reflection in the windowpane and searched her own eyes for the answer to a question she couldn't quite articulate. Was she ready?

Across the city, Arjun sat in the quiet of his study, the same room where he had spent countless nights drafting blueprints and crafting the visions that had become his legacy. Tonight, however, the neatly stacked papers on his desk remained untouched. His gaze was fixed on the small frame that held a picture of him and Meera Jr. taken years ago, her arm slung around his shoulder, her laughter captured in a moment of unguarded joy. He smiled softly, running his thumb over the edge of the frame. Meera Jr. had always been his greatest source of pride, the living embodiment of all he had worked for. And yet, as he sat here tonight, he couldn't help but think of the other Meera—the one who had set him on this path, the one whose name he had carried like a talisman through the years.

Forty years. The weight of it pressed against his chest as he leaned back in his chair. How had so much time passed? The promise they had made felt as vivid as the day it was spoken, yet the man he was now bore little resemblance to the young dreamer who had made it. He had built a life, weathered storms, and found joy in unexpected places, but the memory of Meera Sr. had remained a constant. It wasn't an ache or a longing for what could have been; it was something gentler, a gratitude that had deepened with time. She had shaped him, inspired him, and though he hadn't seen her in decades, she was as much a part of his story as his own reflection. He stood and walked to the bookshelf, his hand hovering over the spines before pulling out a small journal. It was a habit he had never outgrown, writing to her in the quiet moments when his thoughts grew too large to contain. He opened it to the last entry and read the words he had written months ago:

"To the one who taught me to build, not just with stone and steel, but with hope. If we meet again, I will thank you for all that you gave me, even without knowing it."

Closing the journal, Arjun felt a swell of emotion rise in his chest. Tomorrow, he would keep his promise. He had no illusions about what the meeting might bring—he didn't expect rekindled romance or dramatic revelations. What he wanted, more than anything, was to see her, to honor the connection that had guided him through so much of his life. His thoughts were interrupted by a knock at the door. Meera Jr. peeked in, her eyes filled with the warmth and curiosity that had always reminded him of her mother.

"Everything okay, Dad?" she asked, stepping into the room.

Arjun nodded, offering her a reassuring smile. "Just thinking."

She tilted her head, studying him. "You've been quiet today. Is something on your mind?"

He hesitated for a moment, then said, "Tomorrow's an important day for me. Something I've been waiting for a long time."

Meera Jr. didn't press him for details. She had learned over the years that her father had his own way of processing things, and she respected that. Instead, she walked over and gave him a hug.

"Whatever it is, I'm sure it'll go well," she said softly.

As she left the room, Arjun felt a wave of gratitude wash over him. Meera Jr. had been his anchor, his light, and though she didn't know it, she carried within her the spirit of the woman he was preparing to meet.

The night stretched on, long and restless. In their separate spaces, Meera Sr. and Arjun both found themselves revisiting moments from the past, their thoughts weaving a tapestry of memories and emotions. Meera Sr. thought of the first time she had met Arjun, the way his passion for architecture had ignited something in her. She remembered the letters they had exchanged, the plans they had made, and the way life had quietly unraveled those plans. Arjun, too, was lost in recollection. He thought of their conversations about literature and architecture, the way her words had pushed him to dream bigger, to see the world not just as it was but as it could be. He thought of the day they had parted, the promise they had made, and the years that had followed.

Both of them wrestled with the same questions: Would they recognize each other? Would the connection they had shared still exist? And most of all, what would this meeting mean for the lives they had built? As dawn approached, neither of them found solace in answers. But they both felt the pull of destiny, a quiet certainty that tomorrow would mark the beginning of something new, even if they didn't yet know what that would be.

The city stirred with the first light of morning, and with it, the promise of a day that had been forty years in the making. Meera Sr. and Arjun each rose with a mixture of hope and trepidation, their hearts heavy yet full. The time had come.

CHAPTER XXV

THE FIRST GLANCE

Arjun awoke before the sun, the pale light of dawn creeping through the curtains of the house he had built with his own hands. It was a home designed not for himself but for his daughter, Meera Jr., a gift of permanence and love in a life that had often felt transient. Every stone, every corner bore his signature, but the soul of the house belonged to the young woman who had grown up within its walls. It stood in the heart of the city where he had met his, Meera, a quiet nod to the past he had never forgotten. The air that morning was heavy with expectation. He stepped into his bathroom, his reflection staring back at him— a face lined by years of hard work and quiet introspection. The dark hair that once fell messily over his forehead was now speckled with silver, but his eyes, deep and contemplative, still held the same intensity they had in his youth. He ran a hand over the light stubble on his jaw and paused, almost as if he were searching his own gaze for reassurance. Arjun chose his attire with care, his hands steady despite the storm of emotions within him. He opted for a crisp white shirt and a pair of tailored trousers, simple yet timeless. Over it, he wore a navy blazer, the fabric soft against his skin. His daughter had once said he looked most himself in blue, a sentiment that struck him as oddly comforting now. He tied his watch around his wrist, the same one he had worn for decades, a gift from his late wife—a token of time that seemed more poignant than ever today and his prized cufflinks. In the quiet moments before leaving, Arjun found himself drawn to his study, the place where his life's work had taken shape. On the desk lay a collection of sketches, blueprints, and letters—a lifetime of dreams and achievements. His fingers lingered over the edges of an envelope, one of the many he had written to Meera Sr. but never sent. He thought of her now, wondering if she had aged as gracefully as she had lived, if her presence still commanded a room with the quiet strength he had always admired.

Across the city, in a room she had rented for the night, Meera Sr. stood before a mirror, a quiet resolve etched across her features. She had returned to this city for the first time in thirty-five years, the streets familiar yet changed, echoing with memories she had buried deep. The anticipation of meeting Arjun had settled into a steady thrum beneath her ribs, a mix of nervous excitement and the fear of shattering the fragile sanctity of the past. She smoothed the pleats of her sari, its ivory fabric accented with a subtle gold border. It was a deliberate choice, elegant yet understated, much like the woman she had become. Her hair, streaked with silver, was pinned neatly at the nape of her neck, though a few strands fell free, softening her sharp cheekbones. Her eyes, framed by faint lines, held a depth born of years spent navigating the peaks and valleys of life. Meera took her time applying a touch of kajal to her eyes, her movements methodical. She had always been composed, but today, she felt the vulnerability of a woman revisiting a chapter of her life she had long since closed. Would he recognize her? Would she recognize him? The questions tugged at her heart, but she pushed them aside. This meeting wasn't about rekindling anything; it was about honoring what had been, about gratitude for the man who had shaped her in ways even he might not realize. Her gaze wandered to the leather-bound notebook resting on the bedside table. It was filled with poetry and musings, some of them inspired by Arjun, though she would never admit it aloud. She ran her fingers over its cover before tucking it into her bag. **Just in case,** she thought, though she wasn't sure what she meant by it.

As the morning unfolded, the city came alive with its usual rhythms, but for Arjun and Meera, it felt as though time had slowed. Arjun stepped out of his house, the sunlight warm against his face. The streets he drove through were familiar, but today, they seemed imbued with a sense of purpose, each turn bringing him closer to a moment forty years in the making. He arrived at the coffee shop early, his heart beating faster with each passing minute. It was their coffee shop, the place where they had once shared endless conversations about architecture and literature, about dreams and the lives they hoped to build. The building had changed over the years, its facade modernized, but the essence of it remained the same. Arjun chose a corner table by the window, his favourite, the sunlight filtering through the glass, casting delicate patterns on the polished wooden surface. He sat with his hands clasped, his foot tapping lightly against the floor—a small betrayal of the nervous energy he felt. He had asked his daughter to sit a few tables away, her presence a quiet reassurance. She didn't know much, only that this meeting was important to her father, and she had respected his need for privacy. For her even the sudden invitation to come back to the house came as a surprise, but being the doting daughter, she never questioned the will of her father. The minutes stretched, each one heavier than the last. Arjun's mind raced with possibilities. Would she come? Would she be the same Meera he had known, or had time reshaped her into someone unrecognizable? His thoughts oscillated between hope and doubt, his emotions a fragile balance of excitement and fear.

Meera Sr. stood at the entrance of the coffee shop, her hands clutching the strap of her handbag. She had spent the morning walking through the city, revisiting places that held echoes of her past. The streets had changed, yet they felt like home in a way that startled her. The coffee shop was smaller than she remembered, its charm now understated but still warm. She hesitated for a moment, her heart pounding in her chest. She hadn't felt this nervous in years, not even when she had stood on stages accepting accolades for her work. This was different. This was personal. Taking a deep breath, she pushed the door open. The soft chime of the bell announced her arrival, and the hum of conversation quieted for a moment before resuming. She scanned the room, her eyes searching for him, though she wasn't sure what she was looking for.

And then she saw him.

Arjun sat by the window, the sunlight illuminating his profile. He looked different yet achingly familiar, his posture still carrying the quiet confidence she had always admired. His hair was silver now, his face lined with the years, but his presence was unmistakable. He was dressed impeccably, his appearance a mirror of the man she had once known—dignified, thoughtful, and unassuming. For a moment, Meera couldn't move. Her breath caught in her throat, her eyes filling with a rush of emotion she hadn't anticipated. Forty years had passed, and yet, here he was, the same man who had once filled her days with light and possibility.

Arjun felt her presence before he saw her. Something in the air shifted, a current of familiarity that made him turn his head. When their eyes met, the world seemed to pause. Meera stood at the entrance, her sari glowing softly in the morning light. She was breathtaking, her elegance untouched by time. Her eyes met his, and in that moment, the years melted away. The distance that had once separated them was gone, replaced by a connection that felt as strong as it had all those years ago.

Neither of them moved, neither spoke. The moment hung between them, fragile and infinite, a reunion forty years in the making. For Arjun, it was as if the air had been knocked from his lungs. For Meera, it was a quiet affirmation of all the choices, all the paths that had led her here. The coffee shop seemed to fade around them, the noise and movement a distant blur. It was just the two of them, their eyes locked, their hearts full. And as Meera took a step forward, Arjun rose to meet her, the weight of the years carried not as a burden but as a testament to the strength of what they had shared.

The first glance was everything

Between Silence and Secrets

The coffee shop was filled with a gentle hum of life—the soft clink of cups, muted conversations, and the occasional burst of laughter. But for Arjun and Meera, seated across from each other at the small corner table, the world outside their bubble felt irrelevant, a distant echo. For a moment, neither spoke. They simply regarded one another, absorbing the reality of a meeting that had lived in their imaginations for decades. Time had etched its mark on both of them, yet the essence of who they were remained vividly intact. Arjun saw in Meera's eyes the same quiet determination that had once drawn him to her. For Meera, Arjun's presence exuded a calm resolve, his gaze steady but softened by life's trials.

"It feels surreal," Meera said finally, her voice steady yet tinged with emotion.

Arjun smiled, his lips curling into an expression both warm and uncertain. "Surreal, yes. And overdue."

They both laughed softly, the sound breaking the fragile tension that had lingered. Meera adjusted her sari, her hands moving with a composure that belied the storm of emotions within her. Arjun leaned back slightly, his fingers tracing the edge of the ceramic coffee cup in front of him, grounding himself in the tangible.

"How are you, Meera?" he asked, his voice low and measured, as though afraid to ask too much too soon.

"I'm… I'm here," she said with a small, wistful smile. "And that feels like the most honest answer I can give." She met his eyes and found a depth there that mirrored her own. "And you?"

Arjun paused, his thoughts flickering over the years—the triumphs and losses, the choices that had brought him to this very moment. "I'm here too," he said finally, the words carrying more weight than their simplicity suggested.

The conversation started formally, as if they were strangers reacquainting themselves. They spoke of the mundane—how the city had changed, the weather, the familiarity of the coffee shop. But beneath the polite exchange lay a profound understanding, a shared acknowledgment of the years that had shaped them both. Gradually, the formality gave way to something deeper, something unspoken yet ever-present. Meera tilted her head slightly, her gaze softening. "Arjun, tell me about your life. All these years… I've often wondered."

He hesitated, his fingers tightening around the cup before releasing it. "It's been a journey," he began, his voice tinged with a mix of pride and sorrow. "Architecture became my anchor. After we… after life took us in different directions, I poured myself into it. Building something tangible helped me navigate the intangible."

He paused, as if weighing his next words. "I married a wonderful woman. We were happy… for a time. But she passed away far too soon." His voice faltered, the pain of that loss still a tender bruise on his heart. "After that, everything changed. I had to rebuild, not just professionally, but personally. It wasn't easy, but it taught me resilience, how to keep going when all you want to do is stop."

Meera listened intently, her hands resting lightly on the table. "And you did," she said softly, her words carrying an unspoken admiration. "You kept going.

That takes strength, Arjun."

He nodded, a faint smile ghosting his lips. "It does. But I wasn't alone. There were… people who inspired me, who reminded me of the kind of life I wanted to build. People like you, Meera."

She blinked, caught off guard by the quiet sincerity of his words. "Like me?"

"Yes." Arjun met her gaze, his expression unwavering. "I carried you with me, in a way. The ideals you lived by, the things you taught me—about literature, about seeing the world through a lens of possibility. Those stayed with me, even when we weren't in each other's lives."

Meera felt her throat tighten, the weight of his words settling over her. "I… I don't know what to say," she admitted.

"You don't have to say anything," he said simply.

But she did. "You were there for me too, Arjun. Not in person, but in spirit. When I found myself questioning everything, doubting whether I could keep going… I thought of you. Of your quiet determination, your way of finding beauty even in chaos. It gave me strength."

The words hung between them, a bridge across the years. They didn't need to fill the silence that followed; it spoke volumes on its own.

Meera then began to share her story, her voice steady yet tinged with emotion. She spoke of her journey as a writer, the nights spent hunched over her desk, the thrill of her first published work, the challenges of carving out her place in a world that often dismissed her voice. "There were times," she confessed, "when I wanted to give up. But I couldn't. Not when I thought of all the people who believed in me, who had once told me I was capable of more than I knew."

Arjun smiled, his expression one of quiet pride. "You've always been capable, Meera. I never doubted that."

She chuckled softly, a sound that carried both warmth and weariness. "I wish I'd had your certainty. But I suppose that's life, isn't it? Learning to trust yourself, even when it feels impossible."

As they spoke, the years fell away, their connection as effortless as it had been in their youth. They didn't need to say everything—some things were understood in the spaces between their words. The shared glances, the subtle smiles, the way they leaned slightly toward each other as they spoke—it was all a testament to the bond that had endured despite the distance and time.

The conversation drifted to their work, their passions, the lives they had built. Arjun spoke of his designs, how he had tried to create spaces that felt like home, like possibility. Meera shared her joy in mentoring young writers, in watching their voices emerge, unencumbered by fear. They poured their hearts out, not in a rush, but with the ease of two people who knew they would be heard. There was no judgment, no need for explanations—just understanding. The words between them had softened to a steady rhythm, like the rise and fall of waves against the shore. Arjun and Meera spoke of lives lived, paths diverged, and moments that had shaped them, their voices tinged with a blend of nostalgia and quiet gratitude. The air between them was charged, not with the tension of unspoken emotions, but with the reverence of two souls finally laying bare their truths.

As the conversation drifted, Meera mentioned her

writing—a detail she hadn't fully disclosed before. "I've written under a pseudonym for years," she said, her lips curving into a faint smile. "It gave me the freedom to be myself while keeping a part of me hidden."

Arjun tilted his head, intrigued. "A pseudonym? What is it?"

"Ananya," she replied, her voice soft, almost shy. "It was the name of a character I imagined when I was younger, someone who represented the person I wished to be—fearless, resilient, unyielding."

The name struck something deep within Arjun. He leaned back slightly, his expression shifting from curiosity to astonishment. "Ananya..." he repeated, his voice barely above a whisper.

Meera noticed the change in his demeanor. "Do you know the name?" she asked, her brow furrowing.

Arjun nodded slowly, his gaze distant as memories cascaded through him. "The *Will to Move Forward.*" The words came out like a revelation, each syllable weighted with emotion. "That book—it changed me, Meera. I read it during one of the most difficult periods of my life. It felt as though the author knew me, knew the battles I was fighting. I carried its words with me for years, never realizing..." He paused, his voice faltering.

"That it was me?" Meera finished for him, her own emotions wavering.

Arjun nodded, his eyes searching hers. "Your words gave me strength when I needed it most. And now, sitting here with you, it all makes sense—the way it felt so personal, so intimately familiar. It wasn't just a book; it was... you."

Meera's heart swelled with a mix of pride and vulnerability. "I wrote that book because I needed to believe in the message myself. It was a way to hold on to hope, to remind myself of the strength I found in those I admired, in the people who shaped me." She hesitated, her gaze softening. "In you, Arjun."

The weight of her words settled over them, binding them in a shared understanding that spanned decades. But before the silence could linger, Meera spoke again. "You know," she said, her voice tinged with curiosity, "there was something that drove me to finally return to this city, after all these years. I read an article. It was written by someone named Illusion."

Arjun's lips twitched in recognition, but he said nothing, waiting for her to continue.

"It was about an architect," she went on, her voice growing quieter. "Someone who had faced unimaginable loss but had poured his soul into creating beauty, into rebuilding not just structures but lives. The way it was written… I don't know how to explain it. It felt like it was calling me here." She looked at him then, a flicker of realization dawning in her eyes. "That architect… it was you, wasn't it?"

Arjun's silence was confirmation enough. Meera inhaled sharply, her heart catching in her throat. "It makes sense now. The emotion in that piece, the way it resonated with me—it was you, Arjun."

Meera exhaled deeply, her hand brushing away an errant tear. "So much of my life has been shaped by these invisible threads—your words, your actions, even when you weren't physically present. And to think, all this time, our lives have been quietly intertwined in ways we couldn't have imagined."

"It's as though life knew we needed each other, even from afar," Arjun said, his voice warm and steady. "And yet, it gave us the space to grow, to become who we were meant to be."

Meera smiled through her tears, her heart swelling with gratitude. "I've often wondered, Arjun, what my life would have been like if we had stayed together, if things had turned out differently. But now, sitting here with you, I realize—I'm grateful for the way things unfolded. It was your absence, your unspoken presence, that shaped me, that gave me the strength to become who I am today."

Her words hung in the air, a testament to the quiet resilience of their bond. "I loved you, Arjun," she said softly, her voice trembling with both sorrow and acceptance. "And I suppose, in some way, I always will. But it's not a love that longs for what might have been. It's a love that celebrates what is—a love that shaped my life, even in its unrequited form."

Arjun leaned forward then, his eyes glistening with unshed tears. "Meera," he said, his voice low and earnest, "your love—your presence in my life—it's been a gift. A compass, even when I didn't realize it. And while I've carried my own share of questions and what-ifs, I've never doubted one thing: that meeting you changed me, for the better."

They sat in silence for a moment, the weight of their words settling between them. It was not a silence of regret but one of reverence, of acknowledgment for the paths they had walked and the connection that had endured.

Finally, Arjun leaned back, a small, enigmatic smile playing on his lips. "But," he said, his tone lighter now, "there's one question I think you might want answered, You have answered that you loved me, but, Do I still Love you?"

Meera raised an eyebrow, her curiosity piqued.

"Oh?"

Arjun's smile widened, and he turned slightly, raising a hand to beckon someone over. "I think it's time you met someone," he said, his voice filled with a quiet excitement. Meera's eyes followed his gesture, her breath catching as she saw a figure approaching their table. She glanced back at Arjun, her heart racing with a mixture of anticipation and wonder. "Arjun," she whispered, her voice trembling, "what is this?"

But he said nothing, his gaze fixed on her, his expression one of quiet satisfaction. "You'll see," he said simply, his tone filled with a warmth that promised answers and, perhaps, even more.

I Cannot Unlove You

The air between them grew heavier, laden with unspoken questions and emotions as Meera Sr. watched the figure approach their table. The cafe, bustling just moments before, seemed to fall silent, as though the universe itself held its breath in anticipation of this moment. It was her—Meera Jr., the young woman Meera Sr. had met not long ago at the Jaipur Literature Festival. She had felt drawn to her then, captivated by her earnest passion for words, her sharp intellect, and her unmistakable charm. The article Meera Jr. had written had left an indelible mark on her, much like the girl herself. But now, standing in the soft morning light, there was something achingly familiar about her.

Meera Jr. stopped a few feet away, her gaze flitting

nervously between Arjun and Meera Sr., who sat frozen in her seat. A quiet gasp escaped Meera Sr.'s lips as the realization dawned. The similarities were too striking to ignore—the fierce spirit, the writer's intellect, the softness of her eyes, the way she held herself with quiet confidence. The girl before her wasn't just a talented writer or a kindred spirit; she was a piece of Arjun, a reflection of a life he had built without her.

"Meera…" Meera Sr. murmured, her voice trembling.

The younger woman's eyes widened, and she looked at her father for answers, her confusion mirrored by the older woman seated across the table. Arjun exhaled deeply, his hands resting on the table as if steadying himself for what was to come.

"She's… named after me," Meera Sr. finally said, her voice breaking under the weight of realization. "You named her after me."

Arjun nodded slowly, his gaze unwavering as he met hers. "I did," he said simply, his voice low and steady. "She's the best part of me, Meera. The best part of a life I wouldn't have had the strength to live if it weren't for you."

Meera Jr. stood frozen, her expression shifting from confusion to shock as she began piecing together the fragments of the conversation. "Wait," she said, her voice faltering. "What… what's going on here?" Her eyes darted between the two older figures, searching for clarity.

"Meera," Arjun began, addressing his daughter, his voice thick with emotion. "There's something I need to tell you—something I should have told you a long time ago."

The younger woman tilted her head, her brows knitting together. "What is it, Papa?"

Arjun glanced at Meera Sr., seeking her silent permission to continue. She nodded faintly, her hands gripping the edge of the table as if bracing herself for what was to come.

"For years," Arjun began, his voice trembling, "I've carried a story in my heart—a story of a woman who changed my life, who gave me strength when I thought I had none left. That woman…" He paused, his voice breaking. "That woman is sitting right here. She's the one who inspired me to keep going, to raise you, to become the man I am today."

Meera Jr.'s eyes widened, her breath hitching as the weight of his words settled over her. She turned to Meera Sr., her expression a mixture of awe and disbelief. "You?" she whispered, her voice barely audible.

The older woman nodded slowly, tears brimming in her eyes. "I didn't know," said Meera Sr., her voice thick with emotion. "I felt it but could never place it, when I read the article. I didn't know you were… his daughter."

The realization struck Meera Jr. like a bolt of lightning. The woman she had admired, whose work had shaped her own journey, was not just a literary icon but a part of her father's past—a past she had unknowingly carried forward.

"I wrote that article because of you, you inspired me and for my Papa!" Meera Jr. said, her voice trembling. "I never knew… I never imagined…"

The three of them sat in silence for a moment, the enormity of the revelation settling over them like a heavy blanket.

"I'm sorry," Arjun said suddenly, his voice filled with quiet regret. He turned to his daughter first. "I'm sorry I never told you. I thought… I thought it was enough to raise you, to give you a life filled with love and stability. But now I see that I should have shared this part of me with you sooner."

Meera Jr. shook her head, her eyes glistening with unshed tears. "Papa, you don't need to apologize. I understand now. I understand everything."

Arjun then turned to Meera Sr., his gaze filled with a mixture of gratitude and sorrow. "And I'm sorry to you, too," he said, his voice breaking. "I'm sorry for the years of silence, for the things left unsaid. But I want you to know this: Every step I took, every decision I made, was guided by the love and inspiration you gave me. You were always with me, Meera, even when we were apart."

Meera Sr. shook her head, a small, bittersweet smile playing on her lips. "Arjun," she said softly, "there's nothing to apologize for. If anything, I'm grateful—for everything. For the love we shared, for the distance that allowed us to grow, for the lives we've built because of it all. I wouldn't be who I am today without you."

Her words hung in the air, a testament to the unyielding bond that had endured the test of time and distance. Meera Jr., still reeling from the revelations, reached out to place her hand over her father's. "Papa," she said, her voice filled with quiet determination, "thank you—for everything. For raising me, for loving me, for showing me what it means to be strong. And thank you for sharing this part of you with me, even if it took all these years."

Arjun's eyes glistened with tears as he covered her

hand with his own. "You've always been my strength, Meera. Both of you."

The stillness of the moment was broken only by the soft hum of life around them—the clinking of cups, the murmurs of conversation, the distant rustle of leaves in the breeze. But within their small circle, time seemed to stand still, the weight of their shared history binding them together in a way that words could never fully capture. Finally, Arjun stood, pulling Meera Jr. into a tight embrace. He held her as though anchoring himself to the present, to the life he had built, even as the past lingered like a shadow. Then, with his arms still wrapped around his daughter, he turned to Meera Sr., his eyes filled with a quiet, unwavering resolve.

"And to answer your question!"

"You won," he said, his voice steady despite the emotion that laced it. "I cannot unlove you."

Meera Sr. felt her breath catch, her chest tightening as the words washed over her. They were not a confession, not a declaration of longing or regret, but a simple truth—a truth that had shaped both their lives in ways they were only just beginning to understand. Tears streamed down her face, but she didn't bother to wipe them away. Instead, she smiled—a smile filled with gratitude, acceptance, and a love that transcended time and circumstance.

And in that moment, the three of them—Arjun, Meera Sr., and Meera Jr.—stood bound by the invisible threads of love, memory, and connection, their lives forever intertwined.

EPILOGUE

Life has a way of bringing us back to where it all began. We call it fate, we call it destiny, but perhaps it is something simpler: a return to what was left unfinished, a chance to repay what was borrowed from time. In the story of Arjun and Meera, there lies an undeniable truth—love, in its purest form, always finds its way home. It may not look the way we imagined, and it may not unfold the way we hoped, but it returns, as karma, as redemption, as the invisible threads that stitch two hearts together.

Arjun got his return—he reaped what he sowed. He poured his love into the world, into the life of a little girl who became his reason to endure, his reason to grow. His daughter. was the living embodiment of the love he once shared with Meera, a gift he never asked for but one he needed. Through her, Arjun found his purpose, his legacy. But what of Meera? What of the woman who spent decades in quiet solitude, the woman whose heart remained tethered to a love she dared not claim?

Love is not always fair. It gives and it takes; it fulfills and it deprives. Meera was left alone—not because she deserved loneliness, but because life, too often, mirrors the choices we make. She honored her love for Arjun in silence, burying it in her words, in her art, in the life she built with his memory as her guide. But perhaps if she had spoken, if Arjun had dared to ask, their lives would have been different. There would have been no what-ifs, no decades lost to hesitation.

And that is the lesson that lingers: *speak your heart.* Do not let fear hold you captive, do not let the unknown keep you from reaching for the life you deserve. Arjun and Meera were never apart in spirit, but they allowed life to pull them apart in flesh. They let their love become a quiet ache instead of a shared existence. How many of us do the same? How many of us love in secret, hoping time will deliver what courage could claim?

Yet, there is a quiet beauty in what Arjun and Meera shared. Love is not always about being together. It is about honoring the person who shapes you, the one who stays with you even when they are not by your side. Arjun honored Meera in his actions; Meera honored Arjun in her heart. Their love was not a failure—it was a triumph of resilience, of growth, of becoming.

Let their story be a reminder. Do not wait for time to decide your fate. Love is not meant to be contained in what-ifs. Act wisely. Speak your heart. Honor the ones you love while they are here. After all, the only regret that truly haunts us is the love left unspoken.

ACKNOWLEDGEMENT

First and foremost, I would like to express my deepest gratitude to the universe for serving as my guide and illuminating my path. Without its guidance, I would not have been able to navigate the journey that has led me to this point.

I extend my heartfelt thanks to my family and friends, whose unwavering support, boundless love, and steadfast faith in me have been a constant source of strength. Your belief in my abilities has kept me motivated and inspired. A special note of thanks goes to Vinnu, who has been my rock, providing invaluable assistance and being there for me through thick and thin. Your encouragement and support have been crucial in helping me overcome numerous challenges.

Moreover, I am profoundly grateful to all my readers. Your continuous support and the profound love you have shown me have been incredibly motivating. Your enthusiasm and feedback have kept me going, and I am deeply thankful for each and every one of you.

To everyone mentioned and those who have supported me in ways big and small, your contributions have made a significant impact on my journey. I am truly blessed to have such a wonderful network of people in my life. Thank you from the bottom of my heart.

My world revolves around your smile.

Thank you Daddy and Ma for being there and holding my back always.

LOVE YOU ALWAYS!

IN THE END, IS EVERYTHING MEANINGLESS?
Twisted
Love
NAMAN MISHRA